Ladies' Man

An Entertaining Love Novel

I0525695

Frederick Germaine

Presents

Ladies' Man

An Entertaining Love Novel

Copyright © 2011 by Frederick Germaine

Cover Design: www.OmarJones.com

ISBN 978-0-578-07843-4

Dedication

To all the sleepers in life who are afraid of accomplishing their dreams. Remember, nothing comes to a sleeper but a dream. Wake up!

Acknowledgements

First and foremost, I would like to thank God for blessing me with my vision, determination, and drive. Without him, none of this would be possible.

Thanks for all the black women in American and abroad holding it down. Sometimes you don't get the credit you deserve, but we all know you're the backbone and pillar in our society. Love you so much and thanks for all your support!

For all my brothers out there who have been through much trials and tribulation, all I can say is continue to keep your head up! When you're at your lowest point in life and feel you can't make it, remember there's no way but up.

-Frederick Germaine

Contents

Part I

Betrayal

Spring 1993: Los Angeles, California

Chapter 1

It was a brisk and windy evening in late March, and I was walking towards my blue 1978 Datsun B210 right after baseball practice. I was known as, Damien Hardy, a seventeen-year-old senior at Crenshaw High School in South Central Los Angeles. My six-foot one frame complimented my muscular one hundred ninety-five pound build perfectly. Smooth bronzed color skin tone, with straight white teeth, and wavy jet black hair gave me the extra edge of attractiveness others yearned for. Although my peers considered me a black kid, others thought I was from Caribbean descent. Along with my desired physical physique from baseball scouts, I was a high school academic and athletic All-American boasting a 3.75 GPA and .411 batting average simultaneously. Despite all the countless offer letters and courting by college scouts, I decided to stay in my home city and attend the University of Southern California.

"Hey, where do you think you're going, All-Star?" asked Coach Frazier. Coach Frazier was Crenshaw High School's batting coach, who settled back into Los Angeles after a brief stint in the majors with the Los Angeles Dodgers. He gained a lot of respect with the high school players not only because he was a former major league player, but he was a former baseball player from Crenshaw High School about a decade earlier. Coach was my mentor and only father figure in my life.

"C'mon on Coach Frazier," I replied. You know I made plans to visit Crystal at USC this evening."

"Yeah, but I thought you cancelled your visit with your girl to work more on your swinging technique after practice today."

"I decided to surprise her anyway. Besides, I promise to make up our batting session tomorrow."

"Okay, Casanova, but you better be glad that USC scholarship is already in the bank. Otherwise, you would be staying here with me for another hour."

"Thanks a bunch, Coach. I'll definitely stay late tomorrow after practice, I promise."

The sun was setting now and it gave off an orange haze over the Los Angeles skyline. I jumped in my car and took Leimert Boulevard until it turned into West Martin Luther King Boulevard headed towards the USC campus. I was amazed how there was little to no bottleneck traffic especially during this time of the evening. While driving, I passed a park where there were a few kids playing baseball in an old field. The field had little to no grass and the designated home run fence was barely erect. It wasn't the most glamorous field but the kids seem to be happy and enjoying themselves. Quickly, I reminisced how I use to be one of those kids in the park playing ball and even sometimes by myself.

Now all the hard work and dedication had paid off, and I was off to a major university to enjoy something others love to do. I would be the first black male in my family to go to college and earn a degree. I had every intention on obtaining my college degree no matter what curve ball life threw at me. My parents, who were now deceased, always pounded into my head the importance of an education. My grandmother, who was now raising me, always stressed a college degree, is something no one can ever take away from you. I had already made my mind up I would finish college first and obtain a degree before ever considering the professional ranks. It was the least I owed to my parents and grandmother. Besides earning a scholarship to play college baseball, I had managed to stay trouble free and away from the gang life in the streets of South Central Los Angeles. This was no easy task considering I went to a high school where gang activity was synonymous with its location. I realized I was truly blessed and lucky as hell.

While driving my old beat up bucket down the boulevard, I quickly put on the new Tupac cassette called *Strictly 4 My Niggaz*.

Tupac was an up and coming rapper from the bay area gaining much popularity by addressing socially conscience issues in the black community. His lyrics were raw, uncut, and controversial which help led to his new found success. As traffic began to pick up, I began to recite the lyrics from the track "Holla If You Hear Me." "Yeah Pac, spit that shit!" I shouted aloud as I turned up the volume and bumped my head to the beat.

I was on my way to see my girlfriend, Crystal Gayle. Crystal and I had been a dating for almost three years now. When we first met, I was an up and coming all heralded freshman baseball player gaining notoriety in the local press. Crystal was a beautiful standout sophomore cheerleader on the varsity football squad at Dorsey High. She had all the characteristics in a female that turned me on. For instance, Crystal was smart, popular, and attractive in high school. It was her dream to go to USC, complete medical school, and finally open her own medical practice. Her goal of becoming a physician and giving back to people was her passion. She was an ambitious young woman who knew what she wanted in life and how to obtain it.

I finally turn onto West Jefferson Boulevard towards the USC campus and Crystal's off campus apartment. I noticed Crystal had not paged me back. After baseball practice, I paged her and put the code "93" after my own pager number. This was a way we communicated to let each other know that everything was okay and according to plan. Then I quickly remembered I never talked to Crystal since yesterday when we decided to cancel today's visit. I realized how happy she would be seeing me, especially since I was dropping by as a surprise.

While slowly driving through the USC campus, I leaned back further in the driver's seat with my left arm hanging out the window. I still had on my dirty, soiled baseball uniform and figured I could shower and change clothes while at Crystal's apartment. With the music blasting I noticed two cute girls and gave them a wink and a wave. The girls noticed and simply smiled then laughed. I did not flinch but realized the girls were laughing at my adolescence and beat up car. I figured one day I'd have the last laugh once I made it to the major leagues. At that very moment, I slowly continued down the boulevard as if I was a superstar baseball player driving a brand new Benz instead of a bucket.

Dusk finally fell upon the Los Angeles sky when I reached Crystal's apartment. As always, I parked next to Crystal's new till green Nissan 240sx. Crystal's parents had purchased the car for her as a high school graduation present almost a year earlier. She was adamant on the color as she planned to pledge for the local AKA chapter while in college.

Taking my left hand, I opened my car door from the outside to exit the vehicle. Years of wear and tear had taken a toll on the car, and trying to open the door from the inside was too much of a hassle. I slammed the car door shut and made my way up the flight of stairs to apartment 212B. Smiling, I carried a small rose I picked up a day earlier at the Korean grocery store in the neighborhood.

"Crystal, it's me Damien," I shouted while knocking on the apartment door.

Abruptly, I continued to knock on the apartment door when there was no response. I noticed there were aroma therapy candles burning, within the apartment, as I peeked through the half way opened blinds next to the front door. Also, I could hear R. Kelly's latest album called *12 Play* in the background. I thought to myself Crystal must have read my mind and knew I was coming over. Apparently, she was in the shower by now. Before long, I remembered she kept a spare key under the flower pot next to the front door. Quickly, I found the spare key and entered the apartment with the intention of surprising my girlfriend. As I made my way towards the rear of the apartment, I decided to pull off my baseball jersey and join Crystal in the shower. Steadily, I made my way towards her room with jersey in one hand and the rose in another.

"Honey, I'm home," I joked opening up Crystal's bedroom door. Suddenly, what I witnessed was something I could have never imaged in a million years. Simultaneously, I dropped the jersey and rose as my eyes glanced forward.

"Oh my God daddy, I'm cumin on your dick!" Crystal yelled as she rode this stranger's dick with her back towards me.

"That's right baby, cum all on daddy's big black dick," replied the stranger as he slapped Crystal on her ass which was spread all over his pelvis.

"Oh daddy you're fucking my pussy so good!"

"That's what I'm supposed to do. This is daddy's pussy now, right?"

"Hell yeah daddy, this is all your sweet black pussy. All yours, I promise."

I had a bird eyes view and still couldn't believe what I was seeing and hearing. Crystal had her arms wrapped around this strange man's neck while her ass was gyrating up and down on his dick. She was riding him like a top-notch Dallas cowgirl, while he continued to slap her ass with both hands. I knew this guy has to be on the USC football team as his letterman jacket adored a chair next to the bed.

"Crystal, what the hell is going on here?" I shouted over the loud playing music.

"Damien!" yelled Crystal as she turned around and quickly jumped off the football player's dick. She scrambled looking for her robe. "Oh my God, what are you doing here?"

"Who's this clown?" asked the arrogant football player. His head lifted off the pillow momentarily to get a view of me with his dick still on rock hard.

"I thought our love was deeper than this!" I screamed. "I tried to surprise you, and find you up in bed fucking some damn USC football player."

"Hold up partner, you don't even know me," said Mr. Football.

"Nigga you don't know me!" I said continuing to scream. "I got boys on Grape Street that will fuck your shit up!"

"Damien baby, hold up just let me explain everything," exclaimed Crystal. By now she had her robe on and had grabbed my arm. "Aaron and I started out as friends, and I helped tutor him in anatomy class. It wasn't planned I promise."

"Damn it, I don't want to hear anything about an anatomy class," I said. "You two seem to have everything covered regarding anatomy. I gave you three years of exclusive love and this is how you repay me!"

"Baby, please let me finish explaining, it is not what you think," replied Crystal.

"I ought to knock both of you out, but it's not even worth the criminal proceeding," I responded. Plus, I was outsized by Mr. Football who was at least six-foot four and seemed to weigh every bit of two hundred and thirty-five pounds. I quickly picked up my baseball jersey, put it on, and darted out the front door.

"Damien, please don't go!" yelled Crystal as she chased after me.

"Bye, bye lover boy," exclaimed Mr. Football as he lay basking in the silk sheets.

Crystal raced after me down the flight of stairs in her robe, barefoot, and hair in a mess. But it was too late with me being quite the athlete. I had managed to hop in my old bucket and was now turning out the front entrance of the apartment complex. Crystal shook her head, while tears fell quickly down her cheeks. She watched me speed away, and slowly walked back up the flight of stairs to her apartment. Through all of this she kept her stride as the nosy neighbors watch in all the excitement.

"Hey Crystal, where you at?" shouted Mr. Football from the bedroom in the apartment as the front door was wide open. "Get your sexy ass back here on daddy's dick." Apparently, the incident did not faze him one bit.

By now I was on the I-110, driving like a bat out of hell. I didn't realize I had taken the extended interstate route trying to get back to South Central. Zigzagging in and out of traffic, I was trying to make it back to the Crenshaw district as fast as I could. My head was pounding with images of Crystal and Mr. Football, tears were running down my face, and my entire body was in cold sweat. Gathering my thoughts, I decided to slow down in a quick hurry. The last thing I needed before the night ended was the police pulling me over and harassing me for reckless driving or attempting to cause an accident. Without gang affiliations, the Los Angeles County Jail was the last place I needed to be in on this horrible night.

Suddenly, my pager began going off repeatedly. I noticed it was Crystal sending me pages back to back with "911" after her home phone number. I simply picked up the pager and turned it off. Right then there in my car, I vowed never to fall in love again and let a woman manipulate me as Crystal had done. I promised to keep my best interest at heart first if I was to succeed in this cold world. Otherwise, I would be in another dramatic cycle with a woman that could hurt me or couldn't be trusted. The pain and sorrow I felt right then would not allow me to love another woman.

Unbeknownst to me, I had pulled up to my grandmother's driveway a short while after making the silent pack to myself. I quickly wiped away any evidence of tears, from my face, as I didn't want to alarm my grandmother. How could I face anyone, let alone my grandmother, by what I just witnessed? I felt less of a man by the way Crystal had betrayed me.

Just as I began to gain my composure and turn the car off, Tupac's song "Keep Ya Head Up" was playing softly on the cassette I was listening to earlier. "Yeah Pac, thanks for the advise, bro." I said to myself, while looking aimlessly at the car's cassette player. I turned the car's engine off completely. Then I grabbed my glove and bat, slammed the door to the old bucket, and went inside my grandmother's house.

When I walked into the house, there was my grandmother sitting back relaxed in her dilapidated recliner watching an old rerun of *Good Times*. I avoided eye contact and attempted to quickly make it my room. But there was no fooling my grandmother as she had a sense for knowing when something was wrong.

"Hello Damien how was your day?" she asked breaking my stride and turning her head away from the TV for just a moment.

"Oh it was okay, grandma." I replied pausing in the living room while looking down at my glove.

"Is there something wrong with you?"

"No, why do you ask?"

"Because I just sense something is bothering you, Damien."

"I'm just stressed out trying to finish this semester strong and probably have a lot on my plate right now. I guess it all is starting to show."

"Well, the word says do not worry for tomorrow is another day."

My grandmother could recite passages and quotes from the Bible all day long if you let her. So I definitely didn't want to get her started although she meant well.

"Well grandma, I'm going to take a shower and get ready for school tomorrow." I walked over to where she was seated and gave her a goodnight kiss on her cheek. Then I hugged her as I really knew she was truly the only one I loved.

"I just want to tell you how proud I am of you," she said. "And I know your mother and father are looking down from heaven smiling. Boy, you made me so proud of you I don't know what to do. Just remember, when thing are going wrong or not the way you intended he won't forsake you."

"Amen to that," I said. "Well I'll see you first thing in the morning."

"Wait a minute, Damien. You don't want anything to eat?"

"No, I seemed to have lost my appetite."

"I cooked some fried pork chops and smothered them in gravy just the way you like them."

"Thanks grandma, but I can always eat them tomorrow for leftovers."

"Well suit yourself. Good night, baby."

"Good night, grandma," I said as I continued my journey onto my room.

By the time I had finished up with my shower, my soft bed was the best comfort and feeling I had. The incident with Crystal was still surreal as it kept playing over and over again in my head. I laid there with my arms crossed over my chest, looking at the ceiling, contemplating my next move for the future. Whatever I decided would be a hard decision, but I knew it would be something I had to live with for the rest of my life. After a few endless hours of thinking, I finally fell asleep.

Chapter 2

It was 3:20 p.m. the next day, and I was headed towards the school's baseball field for practice. I knew I owed Coach Frazier an extra hour after practice for batting drills. On top of that, the team was preparing to have a strenuous workout as we prepared for a big game against Fremont High School in two days. The baseball uniform I wore was cleaned and pressed by my grandmother the night before. I always wondered how my grandmother went out of her way to make sure it was cleaned to a tee. Especially since my uniform would more than likely be dirty again after the next practice. It must be the love, I thought to myself.

"Hey Coach Frazier, can I talk to you for a second?"

"What's up, Damien? You better make it fast you know the team has a long, hard practice today."

While the other players were running out to the baseball diamond, with their gloves, I tugged on Coach Frazier's arm so we could have more privacy for our conversation. I clearly wanted to be out to everyone's ear path.

"Well Coach, I've been thinking a lot lately on my future and decided I'm not going to USC."

"What!" Coach Frazier shouted. "Boy, what the hell do you mean you're not going to USC? Are you crazy?"

"What I'm trying to say is that I think Los Angeles is not for me anymore right now," I said. "I need to get out and see the world outside of this place."

"Damien, what has happened to you all of a sudden since yesterday to make you want to change your mind and renege on a scholarship to USC?" asked Coach Frazier. "Is Crystal pregnant?"

"No Coach Frazier, she's not pregnant by me."

"Well, what's going on here?" he asked. "I know you don't plan on joining the bullshit military and fight some war overseas."

"No, I don't plan on joining the military either," I replied. "I just want to leave this city. Look around, all you see is melee in Los Angeles. First there was the Rodney King beating, then Latasha Harlins' death, and finally the riots last year. When is it going to stop? I need a change of scenery and a new environment to call home. That's why I've decided to forgo playing baseball at USC and enroll at the University of Miami."

"Miami," responded Coach Frazier. "The University of Miami does not have the exposure and coverage for their baseball program, let alone the talent level. Plus, the school is three thousand miles away."

"I hear what you're saying Coach, but USC has two consensus high school All-American recruits joining their program this fall competing for the starting shortstop position."

"Damien, you know those two recruits pale in comparison to your play and stats. You're a guarantee shoe in for the shortstop position with USC."

"Thanks for the compliment Coach, but my mind is already made up."

"Apparently you have made your decision final, and all I can do now is support you," he said. "Besides, you're coming into full manhood and should make and live with the decisions you select in life. Now you know since you already formally committed to USC you will have to transfer to Miami, and sit out your freshman year due to NCAA eligibility rules."

"Yes Coach, I have that covered too. I spoke to Ms. Jackson, my guidance counselor, this morning and she is preparing all the necessary paperwork. Sitting out my freshman year at Miami, I'll be able to get ahead on academics and beef up in the weight room for the next season."

"Damn it Damien, don't disappoint us. You know Crenshaw High has put a lot of stock into you, and we just want to see you succeed on and off the baseball field."

At that moment, all I could do was give Coach Frazier a hug, with my patented boyish smile, for giving me the support I desperately needed.

Coach Frazier meant more to me than just baseball. He always had my best interest at heart, and helped me to maintain a straight path in life since my freshman year at Crenshaw High. I was damn lucky to have a father figure like him when I needed it the most. It was so unfortunate there were not enough men like him in my community. I found out early in my baseball career, that most coaches only cared enough for you as long as you were hitting grand slams and winning games. But not Coach Frazier, he was always there for me in good and bad times, just as a father would be to his son.

By June, the baseball season was well over and as expected I exceeded my stats from last season. I led the city school district in home runs, batting average, and stolen bases. Even with all my athletic accolades, I graduated from my senior class in the top ten academically. Crystal was all but now a bad memory, and I had long since refused to take her calls at my grandmother's house. I even had my pager number changed so I wouldn't have to deal with her drama. In order to let the past be the past, I had to let Crystal go completely.

I decided to enroll early during the summer semester at the University of Miami, so I could get accustomed to my new surroundings. I wanted to get a jump on my academics as well. Plus, I was itching for a brand new locale as I had never lived outside the 213 area code in my life. Being so far from home was going to be tough, but I was mentally prepared. My grandmother even gave me her blessings and wished me well.

A week before departing Los Angeles, I decided to donate my car to a local nonprofit organization called Homeboy Industries. The organization assisted former gang members and troubled youth turn their lives around. Besides, the '78 Datsun would not fit into the glam and glitz world of Miami, and my grandmother wasn't going to drive it either. My grandmother always taught me to give from your heart and your blessings would multiply. Even though I considered my car a small donation, I knew someone else would be better off with it other than me.

While taking my final drive on the Santa Monica Freeway to donate my car to the nonprofit organization, I noticed the immaculate skyline of downtown Los Angeles in the rear view mirror. I marveled the picturesque city but simply wanted to remember it just at that moment, from my rear view mirror with no regrets.

Part II

The Starting Five

Spring 1998: Miami, Florida

Chapter 3

It was two weeks before the semester ended, and cardboard boxes littered my Coral Gables' apartment. I sat on the sofa reminiscing about the last five years in college. I had procrastinated packing and getting rid of all the junk accumulated in my two-bedroom apartment shared with my roommate. As I sat there listening to the radio which was set to Hot 99 Jams, the latest Trick Daddy song featuring Trina called "Nann Nigga" began to play.

I could not bring myself to believe my college days were all but over. I had been contemplating on what would be my next move in life after college. Apparently, baseball was not in the equation at all. Like most high school All-Americans, my college career was far from stellar and I did not live up to my full expectations or hype. The injury bug was the main catalyst for my lack luster college performance. During my redshirt freshman year, I suffered a rotator cuff tear on my throwing shoulder. Then the following year, I suffered a meniscus tear to my left knee while sliding trying to steal third base. Both injuries ended up being too crucial and my college baseball career suffered. By my senior year, I had a marginal batting average of .233.

As a constellation, Coach Frazier, had managed to call a few of his contacts and got me a tryout with the Atlanta Braves right after the semester ended. The Braves were in spring practice in Jacksonville,

Florida. Even though I had grown an inch and put on fifteen pounds over the last few years, I was looking way past baseball.

Luckily, I had banked on my education just as my grandmother had motivated me to do so. I knew now without an education, I would be another black kid heading back to the ghetto without anything to show from college. Despite my physical setbacks, I managed to obtain a 3.25 GPA and achieve my Bachelor of Science in Business that spring. Since I didn't have a huge family, I opted not to participate in the graduation ceremonies. My education was all that I cared about, and I planned on delivering the framed degree to my grandmother shortly.

Despite my academic achievements at the University of Miami, I remained an unemployed black man in white American. Even though I had a degree, trying to find a job was no easy task as others may have thought it to be. I chuckled to myself, as I remembered getting a call from a recruiter about a month ago. The recruiter stated he found my resume through an on-line job placement website. Once the conversation continued the recruiter stated he was just making a courtesy call with soon-to-be college graduates, and ended the phone call abruptly. After the phone call, I knew I had too much bass in my voice and wasn't exactly what the recruiter was looking for. This overt racism was nothing new to me, especially growing up in South Central Los Angeles. I took it as another challenge and stepping stone in moving forward with my life.

"What's up, room dog?" said a tall dark figure as he entered the apartment closing the door behind him.

"What's going on, Mookie?" I replied. "Where have you been?"

"Oh, just cruising on Ocean Drive at South Beach. I was taking a final peak at the honeys since I'm headed back to Atlanta in two weeks," exclaimed Mookie. "Man, it's hot as a mother fucker out there! I'm definitely not going to miss this damn Miami heat."

Mookie's real name was Darryl Wysinger, and he had been my roommate and baseball teammate for the last five years. He hated people calling him, Darryl, and insisted on being called Mookie instead. His nickname fit his characteristics without a doubt. He always wore a clean bald head which showcased his black cast iron skin complexion. Mookie stood six-foot five, weighed two hundred forty-five pounds, and was ripped like a NFL linebacker. It was by sheer coincidence that Mookie turned down a football scholarship to the University of Georgia. He opted for a starting catcher position on the University of Miami baseball squad. It was his intention on turning pro in a year or two with a lucrative guarantee baseball contract but that never manifested. Despite Mookie being a three sport high school All-American at Southwest DeKalb High School in Decatur, Georgia, he never quite applied himself to his full ability while in college. He never suffered an injury while in college, but his performance substantially failed. I would say the Miami lifestyle got the best of Mookie. When we were freshman, I noticed Mookie was too busy chasing skirts instead of baseballs, but who could blame him with all the sexy women in Miami. By our senior year, Mookie had been kicked off the baseball team due to a second DUI he received. The school allowed him to continue to enroll in class, but that was pointless for Mookie as he had less than half the credits needed to graduate.

"So Damien, you been thinking about what we talked about last week?"

"Thought about what, Mookie?"

"You know moving to Atlanta," exclaimed Mookie. "What else are you looking forward to? Besides, all my homeboys have been telling me Atlanta has changed so much since I have been gone. The '96 Olympics completely reinvented the city."

"How so has the city changed?" I asked while stacking up a pile of boxes next to the front door.

"Well, for one it's a black man's paradise and been deemed the new black Mecca," shouted Mookie as he made his way to the refrigerator and popped open a cold Corona. "Atlanta has gone through this new revitalization process. There's new construction everywhere, jobs, opportunities, and most importantly beautiful black women.

"How could I forget you wouldn't leave out the beautiful black women part," I replied with a grin.

"Well, Damien, with your looks and charisma you could be an instant ladies' man."

"Yeah, from what you're saying, Atlanta may be the move for me. I still have to wait and see how things turn out with my tryout for the Braves in Jacksonville."

"So what's up with you and your cutie Cuban honey on campus with the convertible Porsche?" asked Mookie briefly changing the subject. "Are you still hitting that?"

"Definitely, but it's just plutonic," I replied. "If her rich congressman daddy knew she was screwing a nigga her trust fund would quickly dry up." At that moment we both started laughing.

"Well she ain't got anything on the women in Atlanta just trust me on that one Damien. You can take your pick of thick and sassy or petite and classy. A man like you can definitely keep a starting five."

"So what's a starting five, Mookie?"

"It works just like a basketball game," replied Mookie. "You're the coach and owner while the women are your players who work exclusively for you. You only put your best five starters on the court at any given time. If a player doesn't perform you simply bench her and bring someone else off the pine. If the women get too out of control, you have the power to put her ass on waivers to the next man who wants her. The lovely part about this game is that there is always some eager rookie waiting to showcase her talents and take the place of a veteran. But be careful, rookies can be just as important or detrimental to the team as veterans."

"Mookie, you say some off the wall shit, and that sounds just like a little far fetch fantasy to me."

"I'm telling you, Damien, don't sleep on the starting five concept. For instance, in Atlanta there are ten beautiful black women to every single man. So every man with a little bit of a game can easily have five women on his team. Every woman has specific tasks and roles that set her apart from the other woman on the team. It might be sex, looks, finance, or attitude. Once you get your starting five, you simply name them accordingly to their position and commitment on the team."

"Yeah, I hear what you're saying Mookie, so tell me more." By now I was sipping on a cold Corona with Mookie soaking up what he was telling me.

"It works just like the NBA," he said. "Who would you select as you dream team starting five?"

"You mean my best five players in the league right now?"

"Yeah, nigga, who you got?"

Well, I'd have MJ and Kobe playing the one and two guards. Diesel would be filling up the middle and Barkley as my strong forward with E.J. as my power forward."

"Damn, now that is a dream team," screamed Mookie while continuing to sip on his beer. "You see only the best of the best and only the cream of the crop play on your team. So the same concept applies to women. You dig, bro?"

"Yeah, I dig bro," I replied.

At that moment, I realized Mookie had a sense of street credibility I never noticed before. Sometimes street smarts went much further than anything you could ever learn in a book or class. If I was going to move to Atlanta it would definitely come in handy.

Part III

Welcome to Atlanta

Summer 1998: Atlanta, Georgia

Chapter 4

"Where's gate C37?" I asked the Delta ticket agent nervously, as I was almost out of breath, running up to the counter.

"Straight down on your left, sir," she replied.

I quickly grabbed by book bag and without thanking her ran through the airport terminal trying not to miss my Friday 9:15 a.m. flight. LAX was a madhouse since it was the Memorial Day weekend, and the airport was full of passengers trying to make their flights. The summer had now officially begun.

"Wait, wait, I'm here!" I shouted to the airline boarding agent as she began to close the door leading to the plane. With my ticket and id in hand, I handed both of the items to her still trying to carry my book bag with my free arm.

"Glad you could make it, Mr. Hardy. Enjoy your flight to Atlanta," replied the boarding agent as she torn part of my ticket off and handed my id back to me. She simply smiled and motioned for me to enter the corridor leading to the plane.

As I quickly made my way down the walkway to the plane, I wiped the sweat beads off my forehead and began to smile. "Whew, thank God I made it," I said to myself. Once inside the plane I looked at my ticket and tried to locate my seat. People were still placing their carry-on bags into the compartments over the seats which made it difficult to maneuver down the aisle. Finally, I found my seat which was located near the rear of the plan. Lucky for me, I had a window seat.

"Excuse me, I just need to get to my window seat," I said as I moved passed a bald gentleman and middle aged woman who were sitting by my seat. Both of these individuals were white and stuck out like a sore thumb on the trip to Blacklanta.

"Can you get by young man?" asked the woman who sat in the middle seat as she turned her legs inward.

"Ah, yes now I can. Thank you ma'am," I responded as I took my seat next to the window.

I quickly placed my book bag underneath my seat but not before taking out a travel size bottle of scope from it. The bottle had been emptied earlier and replaced with Absolute Vodka. Despite all the countless road trips on the baseball team, I was always nervous when it came to flying. A shot of vodka always seemed to calm my nerves right on the spot. I quickly opened the scope bottle and downed the contents on my parched throat. The middle aged woman looked at me like I was crazy. She had no clue I had just swallowed a shot of vodka. I then gave a light burp, fasten my seatbelt, and rested my head on a pillow while gazing out the window.

"Good morning passengers, and welcome to Delta flight 3637 bound for Atlanta today," exclaimed the pilot over the intercom system. "We expect a smooth three and a half hour non-stop flight, and hope you enjoy your accommodations. By the way, the high in Atlanta today is expected to reach ninety-five degrees and we should arrive in Atlanta at 3:45 p.m. Eastern Standard Time. Enjoy your flight!"

By the time the plane took off the vodka had penetrated my blood stream, and I was feeling the results. I now had a cool and relaxed emotion over my entire body. I was not a big drinker, and any slight bit of alcohol usually had an effect on me.

While up in the air, I closed my eyes and attempted to take a nap before my arrival in Hotlanta. I thought how my life was changing hopefully for the best. Over a month ago, I finally graduated from college and traveled north of Miami to Jacksonville, Florida. There I failed miserably at the Braves training camp for free agents. The injuries I sustained over the last few years took their toll on my body. I just wasn't the same quick and agile player I used to be. But I accepted it with dignity and knew life must go on. After the training camp ended, I bowed out gracefully and thanked the Braves for the invitation. Luckily, for me I still had my college degree to fall back on.

Before returning back to Los Angeles from Jacksonville, I decided to hook up with Mookie in Atlanta and check out the scenery. Mookie's street credibility and notoriety went along way in Atlanta.

While I was there he was able to get me an interview with Macy's at South DeKalb Mall. His cousin was a sales manager in the ladies' shoes department. To no surprise, I was offered a full time job paying eight dollars an hour plus commission. I eagerly took the menial job knowing I just needed something to hold me over until I landed a job in my career field of business.

Mookie even managed to hook me up with an apartment complex near the mall on Candler Road. It didn't have all the luxuries I wanted, but it was a modest place just to start out in. Apparently, the office manager and Mookie went to high school together. She was able to over look my credit rating and income while approving me for the apartment.

During my short stay in Atlanta, I even met Mookie's mom who extended her southern hospitality to me. She allowed me to stay at her home for the few days I was in town. Mookie was staying with his mom as well, until he found a job and could get on his feet. It was so nice to put a face to a name as he always talked positively about his mom while we were in college. Oddly enough, she raised him independently after his parents divorced when he was just five years old. He never really talked about his father too much but did somewhat resent the fact he never came by to visit or see him play sports while growing up.

After my brief visit to Atlanta, I flew back to Los Angeles to hand deliver my framed college degree to my waiting grandmother. She was elated and cried tears of joy telling me how proud she was. While I was in Los Angeles, I noticed nothing had changed a bit since the five years I had been gone. The hood was still the same with gang members still killing each other and no opportunities for the youth. My grandmother even encouraged me to move to Atlanta and get a new start in life. She even heard Atlanta was a black Mecca full of opportunities. As for Crystal, my grandmother said she would periodically call and ask about me. Crystal had graduated from USC and was now enrolled in their medical school program. Grandma would sometimes pry asking "whatever happened to you two?" But I would just tell her "it just didn't work out."

As the pilot's smooth voice came over the intercom system again, I suddenly awoke from my nap. The plane had landed and we were pulling up to the terminal. All the passengers were anxious to get off the plane as the flight was well long enough. Even the couple sitting next to me had their seatbelts unbuckled, awaiting the plane to stop. As I yawned and stretched out my cramped legs I looked out the window and read the landmark Delta sign stating: Welcome to Atlanta. I thought to myself today was the beginning to the rest of my life.

Chapter 5

I walked briskly through the airport terminal headed towards baggage claim. As I was walking, I quickly noticed a plethora of beautiful black women coming and going throughout the airport. Visually, I picked out my starting five and chuckled to myself thinking of Mookie. Suddenly, I remember to find a pay phone so I could call Mookie letting him know I had arrived in Atlanta. After locating a pay phone no one was occupying I dialed his home phone number.

"Hello," said the deep voice on the other end.

"What's up Mookie? It's Damien."

"What's up my nigga! You made it to Atlanta?"

"Yeah, I just arrived a few minutes ago. I'm headed to baggage claim now."

"Okay, I'm leaving my mama's house right now in Decatur. I'll be there in about twenty-five minutes. What are you wearing?" he asked.

"I'm in a Dodgers baseball cap, baby blue polo golf shirt, khakis, and a pair of Chuck Taylors," I yelled through the phone over all the noise in the airport.

"Ah shit now, nigga. You're going to have to let all that damn L.A. gear go now that you're in the A-T-L."

"Man you know L.A. is where my roots are planted, it's gone but never forgotten," I said smiling. "So what kind of car will you be in?"

"I'll be in my mama's red Cadillac Deville," replied Mookie. Just be on the outside of Delta's baggage claim so I can circle around until I see you."

"Okay Mookie, sounds good. Peace."

"Peace, bro."

I jumped on the terminal train within the airport so I could arrive at the baggage claim quicker. As I exited the train, I travel up a flight of escalators to my final destination. It seemed liked a million people were waiting for their bags on this busy Memorial Day weekend. Bags were circulating on the carousel with anxious passengers grabbing them up. Finally, my two luggage pieces came up and I grabbed them making my way to the exit doors.

It had been nearly thirty minutes since I called Mookie as he pulled up to the curb of baggage claim like clockwork. I signaled for the red Cadillac but Mookie already saw me and moved closer to my direction, stopping right by me. He exited the vehicle and we both gave each other dap and a hug. After that, Mookie picked up my bags as if they were paperweights and placed them in the truck of the car. We both then got into his car.

"Damn Mookie, you drinking already?" I asked as I noticed a strong scent of cognac aroma inside the car.

"Yeah, just a little bit," Mookie replied as he grasps the glass next to the drivers' console and finished the remaining corner of Hennessey. "Besides I'm a veteran, I got this rookie."

"Alright Mr. two DUI's or should I say veteran," I said while shaking my head. "Just be careful you know 5-0 is hot out here especially since it's the Memorial Day weekend."

"So you got your apartment all set to move in?" Mookie asked quickly changing the subject and pulling out into the merging traffic.

"Everything is all set, I just have to pick up my key and pay the rent by six o'clock today," I exclaimed. "I called the office manager yesterday from L.A. to verify everything."

As we pulled up into more traffic, a man in a grey airport uniform yelled at the car "What's up Mookie!"

"You got it pimp!" shouted Mookie back to the man as our car moved on.

"Who's that Mookie?"

"That's just an old partner of mine. We used to play football together back in the day at Southwest DeKalb High."

As we travelled north on I-85 I noticed how vibrant the Atlanta skyline looked in the foreground. Although its size was smaller to Los Angeles it had its own identity. Then Mookie took an exit which placed us on I-20 eastbound towards Decatur. The heat in Atlanta caused mirages on the interstate while we traveled. Coming from Los Angeles, I always associated heat with death. The summer months in Los Angeles were always full of death. Hopefully, Atlanta would be a slower pace than Los Angeles.

Finally, I saw the Candler Road exit and Mookie slowed down but made a swift turn towards the exit. As we waited at the top of the exit for the light to change, I noticed how the area reminded me of South Central but on a smaller scale. There were liquor stores, check cash establishments, pawn shops, and beauty supply stores lined up along the road. When the light turned green Mookie turned left, traveled about half a mile, and pulled into the complex where the sign read King Glen Apartments. I walked inside the office, paid my rent and received the keys to my modest apartment. It would be a long weekend as I didn't have to report to work until Tuesday morning. Until then, I planned to get accustomed to Atlanta, find a set of wheels, and get furniture for my place. Of course, this all included the help and wits of Mookie.

Chapter 6

It had been a little over a month now that I had been in Atlanta. I had yet to secure a job in my career field but continued to network on my off days. I followed up with placement companies, recruiters, and even pounded the pavement searching for a better opportunity. By summer's end, I was determined to have a new job. Working at Macy's for eight dollars an hour plus commission just didn't cut it, but it would do for now.

In the interim, I did manage to buy a car, with the help of Mookie, of course. He turned me on to a car dealership called Jordan Auto's. It was Black owed and located in the hood but had decent cars for a competitive price. Proudly, I purchased an '88 Nissan Maximum for only four grand. The vehicle was in excellent condition with a lot of miles, and it would serve its purpose for now. My dream of one day having a BMW seven series would come soon enough.

I quickly found out early in Atlanta that the car you drove was a status symbol. Most brothers thought if you had a nice car, it was a free pass to pussy. They would live with their mama and not pay rent just as long as they could afford a luxury car. What they didn't know was that ninety percent of the women out there knew whether or not they were going to give you some within the first fifteen minutes of meeting you. And most of the time, the car you drove had nothing to do with it.

As for apartment furniture, Mookie came to the rescue on that issue also. I ended up shopping at a furniture store on Candler Road that was owed by a Korean family. For now, I didn't have a lot of money to buy anything expensive, so I opted to just purchase something decent. As long as people had something to sit on in my apartment, I was satisfied. Anyway, accessories usually help spruce up your furniture, so I invested an effort in that area as well.

After purchasing my vehicle and furniture for my apartment, my savings were now depleted. It helped that my grandmother gave me some extra expense money as my graduation present. Moving to Atlanta cost me more than I thought it would, but I thanked God at least I had a job now to pay the rent.

Chapter 7

It was set to be another record breaking day in Hotlanta. The weather report stated the temperature was to reach ninety-eight degrees, and it wasn't even July yet. But that didn't bother me too much, as I was under the cool confines of the air-conditioning working at Macy's. On this particular day, right around 10:00 a.m., I was attempting to look busy by straightening the Coach shoe display for the third time. Macy's was having a pre-Fourth of July sale, and everyone was anticipating today as high volume, especially with all the great deals on ladies' shoes.

Besides the anticipation of having a great commission day, I was gearing up for Mookie's birthday party as well. Mookie had called me a few weeks earlier, telling me he would be celebrating his twenty-third birthday at the famous Club 112 off Cheshire Bridge Road in Atlanta. He had reserved a VIP section in the club and planned to do it up on his birthday. Ironically, his birthday was on the Fourth of July, but he didn't have even an ounce of patriotic emotion. He always concluded that the holiday didn't signify any importance to black people in any form or fashion. "Hell, we weren't free in 1776 when the Declaration of Independence was signed," he often said.

"Hey Mr. Mann, you got this in a size seven?" asked a female shopper with a sexy voice.

As I turned around quickly from the Coach display, I promptly noticed a beautiful young lady standing in front of me. She had a caramel complexion and stood no more than five-foot four and this was with the three-inch heels she was wearing. Complementing her heels was a tight mini-skirt that seemed to fit her thick ass to a tee. Her halter top showed her full chest, which had to be at least a 36D, and her nipples were also penetrating the fabric. She was showcasing her big, gold hoop earrings, and her long, blond weave was styled just right. She held the display shoe in one hand while twirling her hair with the other hand and chewing on a piece of bubble gum. She displayed an attitude that I liked.

"I'm sure I have your size," I replied as I gently took the shoe she was holding out of her hand. It was a new Gucci strap up heel that had come in a few days earlier.

"Well, I just left Macy's at Lenox Square, and they checked the computer system, which showed this store had my size," exclaimed the pretty young lady, with a bit of an attitude.

"Okay sweetheart, feel free to have a seat and make yourself comfortable as I go check our stockroom," I said, trying to ease any tension she may have. "Oh, and by the way, I'm Damien."

"Nice to meet you Damien, I'm Renee, but everyone calls me Diamond Princess."

"You mean like Trina?" I replied.

"Hell no! Like me," she said with a quick shake of her head. "I made that trick famous."

At that moment, we both burst out laughing, and I knew the ice was broken between us. Besides her pleasing looks, she seemed to have sense of humor, which went a long way in my book. So I quickly retrieved the Gucci shoes from the stockroom and returned.

"Here you are, sweetheart, just as I promised. Do you want to try them on?

"No need Mr. Mann...um, I mean Damien. If they're a size seven, then they fit." By now, Diamond was smiling and batting her long fake eyelashes at me.

"Cool, I'll get you checked out right over here, Diamond." As we made our way over the register, I continued to make conversation as I couldn't let her slip through my fingers now. "So Diamond how does a beautiful young lady, like you, occupy her time in the city of Atlanta?" I couldn't help but notice how her beauty resembled Halle Berry with the body of Pam Grier.

"Well, for one, I'm currently a student at Spelman College with about a year left before I graduate with a degree in business," she replied. "Plus, I dance at the Gold Club to help offset my tuition and living expenses."

"What a coincidence, I just graduated from the University of Miami in April with a degree in business," I exclaimed. "I'm just working here until I find something in my career field."

"Yeah, Damien, I figured you as a corporate type, crunching numbers for some firm downtown."

"Well, since we have so much in common we should get to know each other better," I said. "Besides, I'm new to the area, and maybe you can show me around your city."

"I'm actually from the South Side of Chicago," replied Diamond. "But we can definitely see each other soon." She then reached into her petite Prada purse and quickly scribbled on the back of a business card and handed it to me. "Here's my address and phone number. I live in the Grandview, which is a high-rise condo building in Buckhead. Come by tomorrow night. It's the only night I have off during the holiday weekend. We can chit-chat more then, as I have to go now."

Diamond promptly pulled four crisp hundred-dollar bills from her purse and paid for the Gucci shoes without a hitch. I gave her change back to her and placed the shoes in a shopping bag. She winked at me with a seductive smile and turned away as I eyed her thick ass shaking while she departed.

"Hello sir! Do you have this shoe is a size ten and extra wide?" shouted an obese customer holding up a shoe and snapping me out of my daze.

Apparently, I had been watching Diamond walking out of the store for too long and was still mesmerized by her beautiful figure. But who could blame me, because women like her hardly ever came into our store. I even noticed one of my male co-workers watching her walk away too. He even had a smile on his face as I was pretty sure he was dreaming what he would like to do with her.

"Sure ma'am, I'll go check for you right away," I replied as I went off to the stockroom to hunt for another shoe.

Chapter 8

It was 11:30 a.m. the next day, and I was hyped about going to work. I had to be at Macy's by noon and knew today would be another great commission day. I estimated I earned almost three hundred dollars alone in commission sales yesterday. The sales and upcoming holiday definitely were contributing factors.

Just as I grabbed my car keys and headed out the front door to my apartment, my cell phone rang. The phone display showed a 213 area code which meant the caller was from Los Angeles. Since I only had my cell phone for a short while now, I wonder who was calling me from my home city and with a number I didn't recognize. Suddenly, I quickly thought about my grandmother and hope nothing terrible had happened to her.

"Hello," I said as I answered the phone cautiously.

"Is this Damien?"

"Yeah, this is Damien. Who is this?"

"Hello Damien, it's your cousin Ralph but everyone calls me Raphael now."

Ralph, or better yet Raphael, was my first cousin from Los Angeles. Our fathers were brothers and we both graduated from Crenshaw High School back in '93. Raphael was a shy, introvert, in the closet gay guy. A lot of people attempted to pick on him while we were in school. Since I was a well known jock and had a lot of juice people eventually stayed cleared of him once they found out we were related. Besides, we were blood and I couldn't let people pick on him simply because of his sexuality. Right after high school he moved to San Francisco to what he said was to find himself. Later word got out that since moving to San Francisco, he was out the closet and flaming hot for the entire world to see. Apparently, he now had no concessions on who knew about his sexuality and wanted to fault it for everyone.

"Raphael, whatever happened to Ralph, and why the name change?"

"Well Damien it's my new identity and who I actually am."

"Okay Raphael, I can only respect that. So you back in L.A. now?"

"Yeah, I moved back to L.A. a few months ago. I ran into grandma who told me you had finished college and was now living in Atlanta. That's how I obtained your cell number."

"So how's life been treating you?" I asked.

"It's been good and I can't complain. While in San Fran, I finished cosmopolitan school and met a wonderful mate. He took me out of my shell and rocked my world at the same time boo boo," exclaimed Raphael. "As a matter of fact, he and I traveled to Atlanta a few years back. We went to a gay club in midtown where we befriended a fine down low brother and had an awesome threesome afterwards."

"Ok cousin, now that's too much information for me," I said while laughing a little. "So what are you doing now?"

"My companion in San Fran fizzled out so I'm back in L.A. working in an upscale salon. Honey, I do makeup and hairstyles for rich bitches and celebrities."

"Well Raphael it was good hearing from you, but I got to go as I'm headed to work now. I'm working in the ladies' shoes department at Macy's in South DeKalb Mall."

"Well take care Damien, I'll call you the next time I plan to visit Atlanta."

"Peace Raphael and take care. We'll catch up on the past later."

"Chow," he said.

It was another packed afternoon once I arrived for work at Macy's. All the young girls and hoochies were buying sandals to show off their fresh pedicures on their sexy feet. The conservative business women were grabbing up pumps for their upcoming business trips. It was like Christmas in July as I knew I had to get the free fall money as my commission days would not last forever, especially once the holiday was over. On this particular day, I was so busy, I lost track of time and realized it was already 4:00 p.m. and I didn't have a bite to eat all day. My work shift ended at 7:00 p.m. so I decided to grab a bite to eat in the food court and return for the evening rush.

Prior to going to the food court for lunch, I decided to make a mad dash for my car where I left my cell phone. I needed to check my voicemail messages for the day. To no surprise, the heat outside was intense. I darted for my car parked in the employee's parking section directly in the sun. At this point, I was sweating as I opened my car door, quickly started the engine and turned the air condition on full blast. Then I retrieved my cell phone from the glove box and noticed I had two voice mail messages.

The first message was from Mookie. He stated he called to confirm his party was at squared away at Club 112 in two days. He also mentioned he had the VIP room reserved and had a few strippers that would be showing up too. Right then, I knew he wanted his birthday party to be one to remember forever. When I got to the end of his voice mail message I already knew he had been drinking but brushed it off as Mookie being himself. I figured I'd call him later about my upcoming date with Diamond.

The second message was from a Mr. Richmond, with the marketing department at Coca-Cola. He called stating he received my recently faxed copy of my resume for an entry-level marketing specialist position and was inquiring if I was still interested. He was departing the office today and would be back after the Fourth of July holiday but he wanted me to still return his call ASAP. I quickly listen to the voice mail again smiling, and then dialed Mr. Richmond's contact number. Not surprisingly, I got his voice mail but did leave him a message I was still interested in the position with Coca-Cola and would await a return call from him.

After listening to both messages I realized I needed to confirm my rendezvous with Diamond tonight. As I retrieved the business card she previously gave me, I dialed her phone number which was 404-777-9311 and waited for a response on the other end.

"Hello," answered Diamond.

"Hello sweetheart, it's Damien, from Macy's," I stated. "How are you doing today?"

"Hey baby, I was just thinking about you," she said. "I'm doing well now since you called."

"Oh okay, that's cool. Glad to know I'm still on your mind. You still want me to come by tonight?" I asked.

"Yes baby, I still want you to cum tonight. Don't you want to cum tonight Damien?"

I smiled brightly and chucked to myself internally as to not let Diamond know she caught me off guard with her sexual comment. She said it with a sense of attractiveness, and I was in awed.

"Yes, Diamond, I'm sure you won't have any problems in that area."

"That right, Damien, I've been known to please a few. So baby what time are you coming by tonight?" Diamond asked as she shifted the conversation gears.

"Well, I'm at work right now and don't get off until seven," I replied. "I should be able to get to you around nine-thirty."

"That's perfect I got off work early this morning, but I should be charged up and ready for you tonight baby. See you then, Damien."

"See you later, sweetheart."

As I turned the air condition off in the car I thought to myself "I'm fucking tonight!" Then I prepared mentally for the blazing heat that awaited me once I opened my car door. After exiting my car, I locked the door and ran back into the mall. The one hour timeframe I had for lunch was almost gone, but I still needed to get something quick to eat. Even though I wasn't playing baseball anymore, I still was health conscience about my physique. I scoped the food court then opted for a twelve piece hot wings and fries combo. The line was long but the wings were always worth it. I noticed there wasn't a white person in line just brothers and sisters. And of course, the Asians were cooking and taking orders left and right. Even though Atlanta was suppose to be an all Black city, the Asians still had control on some of the things we loved like hot wings. Hell, there wasn't too much the Asians didn't control in South DeKalb Mall.

When my wing order finally came up, I quickly sat down in the food court to eat my meal. I devoured the wings and fries like it was my last meal, then washed it down with pink lemonade. The fried food guilt hit me as I walked briskly back to Macy's. I quickly felt my rock hard abs and assured myself one meal wouldn't ruin them.

As I reached the sales floor it was packed as when I left an hour ago. All my co-workers were busy helping customers eager to try on shoes. It was right at 5:00 p.m. and I knew my last two hours would be busy. It was Thursday evening and the Fourth of July was on Saturday. Everyone was trying to catch the sale and buy shoes to match their outfits or impress someone. Besides, no one wanted to wait for the last minute and couldn't find their size or style of shoe.

Before I knew it 7:00 p.m. had arrived and I was anxious to clock out as my hot date with Diamond awaited me. I had the next three days off and all my co-workers couldn't believe it. I deserved it as I had been working like a Hebrew slave for the last ten days straight without a day off trying to make rent. My sales manager wanted me to enjoy the sights and sounds of Atlanta during the Fourth of July holiday. The fact that she knew Mookie personally did help too and she wanted me to enjoy his birthday party also. She was always smiling and very cordial when she saw me. I think she had a crush on me, but she had to be at least twenty years older than I was. Mookie always teased me about that situation and told me I should hit it, but I reluctantly told him I don't eat and shit in the same place. It never works.

Before I left work, my co-worker Milton, gave me driving directions to the Grandview. Milton was a local kid who was no more than a year removed from high school. He worked at Macy's part time and was enrolled at Georgia State University as a pre-law major. I guess you could say I was somewhat of his mentor as he learned the pros and cons of college life. Milton told me my friend had to be well-off as only rich white folks lived in the Grandview.

As I exited the mall and made my way to my car, I noticed how the heat and humidity was still unbearable. I thought to myself today was a good day. My date with Diamond was secured for the night, I had a potential job interview lined up, and I made over and beyond my commission goal for the week. Cruising down Candler Road, headed to my apartment, I was smiling from ear to ear. The day wasn't even over yet as the best part was still to come.

Chapter 9

As I looked at my watch, I noticed it was already 9:00 p.m. Within the last two hours, I managed to shave and shower. "Oh shit," I said to myself. "I'd better get out of here before I'm late." Grandma always taught me to be punctual for everything in life no matter what. So I tried to live by that motto alone. She always said, "Black folks feel they can be late for everything in life and think it was fine."

While looking in the wall mirror, I tucked in my baby blue stripe Ralph Lauren golf shirt into my taupe colored slacks. Quickly, I slipped on my argyle socks followed by my Cole Haan burgundy loafers and same color belt. Then I sprayed down my body with Romance cologne which seemed to always smell great with my body chemistry. Mookie always used to tease me in college about my preppy style, stating I looked as if I was going to a model shoot instead of class. But I didn't care as I wanted to be different, and the thug look did me no justice.

Before long I was on I-20 westbound headed towards the Buckhead district of Atlanta. I proceeded to move onto I-85 north, and then took GA 400 to Lenox Road. While waiting for the light to turn green at the intersection of Lenox and Peachtree Road, I couldn't help but notice the area was so clean compared to where I lived. There were also BMW's and Mercedes' driving up and down the intersection. The light finally changed and I made my trek to the Grandview. As I pulled into the visitor space, in the parking garage, I put a piece of peppermint into my mouth. Then I exited my car and headed towards the building entrance and looked right at my watch which showed 9:30 p.m. As I made my way through the revolving door, an attractive young concierge greeted me promptly.

"Hello sir. You must be Damien."

"Why yes, I am."

"Ms. Renee was right you are easy on the eyes."

I smiled and nodded as to thank her modestly for the compliment. Apparently, Diamond had given the concierge my description prior to my arrival.

"You may proceed to the elevators, which are straight to your left sir. Enjoy your stay as well."

I thanked her and gladly made my way to the elevators. As I entered, I pushed the button for the twenty-ninth floor and relaxed to the smooth music playing softly. All I could think about was that Diamond was either making a boatload of money dancing, or someone in her family had deep pockets. While continuing to travel upwards, it really didn't matter to me as all I could think about was Diamond's sexy ass. Suddenly, I began to get a hard on, and the elevator stopped as I had reached my destination. Exiting the elevator, I quickly found my way to unit 2945. Before ringing the doorbell, I made sure my hair was intact, smoothed out my goatee with my fingers, and took a quick look at my outfit. I did all this as if I was in front of a mirror. Then I proceeded to right the doorbell.

After a few moments Diamond came to the door as expected. "Hi baby, glad you could make it," she said. "Come on in."

She was dressed as provocatively as I could only imagine. Her sexy negligee showed a hint of her fatal package, plus she had the matching sheer see-through robe on as well. Her outfit was screaming Victoria Secret, and to top it off she was wearing the Gucci heels I sold her the other day. Of course, Diamond made the outfit look sexy and classy at the same time without looking whorish.

As she led me to the living room, of her condo, it was decked out just as I thought it would be. You can kind of tell how well someone lives by their appearance and demeanor. Her place complimented her looks very well. There were no lights on but there must have been at least one hundred lit candles of all sizes all over the place. Her furniture had a contemporary theme and looked high end from what I could see of it. The floors to ceiling windows were without any window treatments which allow us to view the entire Buckhead district plus a hint of the downtown skyline. To say the least the view was majestic and romantic at a minimum. To top it all off, she had some old school Isley Brothers playing in the background to set the mood right. Diamond led me to the plush leather sofa where we both took a seat. By now I had given her a compliment on her nice place and wardrobe. I noticed she already had a cocktail on the end table to help her relax.

"So what do you want to drink, baby?" Diamond asked. "I have a little bit of everything."

"I'll have whatever you're drinking," I replied. Since I wasn't too big of a drinker, I figured she was drinking light.

"Okay another thug passion for you too," she exclaimed. "You know Tupac said it makes the love last all night."

"Yeah, that's what I heard," was my reply as we both laughed. I glanced at her fine ass shake as she walked over to the bar to make my drink. Then she returned back to the sofa with my concoction and sat right up under me with her legs crossed.

"So I hear you playing that old school love making music by the Isley Brothers," I said. "What do you know about that old school music, youngster?"

"No, the question is what you know about that music baby?" she asked. "Actually it's an old school love mix cd with all the greats like Marvin, Al, Teddy, Rick James, and a few others. My dad is a music connoisseur and musician. He had me listening to all the old school greats when I was growing up. Plus, the music eases tension and helps me relax."

For the next thirty minutes or so we talked about our similarities and differences. We laughed and drank thug passion while our tongues became loose along with other things. Then in an instant it was on. Our eyes met and we both knew it was time for some hot passionate sex. I could only imagine how good she was going to suck my dick as a good blow job was a prerequisite to great sex for me. At that moment, I placed my left hand around her neck and pulled her face closer to mine. I told her to just relax and let me kiss her beautiful lips softly. My lips embraced her top lip then her bottom one. Simultaneously, we both opened our mouths and I placed my tongue on her while kissing her gently. At the same time, my right hand was rubbing down her thigh and I motioned for her to open her legs. Her negligee was crotch less and I began to rub her clitoris smoothly as she moaned. Diamond stopped kissing me briefly to let me know I was rubbing her clit so good and it was making her hot. I smoothly moved my index and middle fingers and played with her juicy thick pussy lips. Her pussy was now wetter than ever, and she was begging for me to fuck her. I wanted the foreplay to last a bit longer as I wanted Diamond to be at her best sexual peak when I entered her. Right then I stood up and took off my shirt. She stood up next to me and slipped off her negligee. There she stood in front of me as fine and sexy as I could have imagined with no wrinkles and the perfect dimensions. Before she attempted to take off her Gucci heels, I told her to keep them on as they made her look even sexier. She began to kiss my nipples and make her way down to my abs and belly button. My dick was rock hard by now and I was demanding she place me in her mouth. With no hesitation, she squatted on the floor and unbuckled my belt. Once my slacks and boxers were down she took one hand and groped the base of my hard dick and entered me with her mouth. She continued to stroke my dick and use her other hand to massage my balls so they wouldn't be jealous. As I briefly opened my eyes to watch her please me, she was looking directly at me also.

"Damn Diamond, you're sucking my dick so good."

"That's what I'm supposed to do baby," she responded as she paused long enough to answer, then placed me back inside her warm mouth.

Right then she stood up from her balancing act of squatting while sucking my dick and pushed me violently on the leather sofa. She turned opposite of my direction and placed her thick ass in my face for the classic sixty-nine position. While she continued to swallow my hard dick, I slapped and rubbed her ass as it shook like Jell-O. Then I commenced to eat her wet pussy as she continued to moan and groan. Just as I took my index and middle finger to play with her clit earlier, I inserted those same fingers into her asshole and stimulated an ass fucking. I used my other free hand to spread her ass cheek while continuing to lick her clit then maneuvered my way down to her pussy lips.

"Oh Damien baby how did you know I liked my asshole played with?" Baby you got me so wet I want you inside me with this thick hard ass dick! Do you want to cum in my mouth first?

"Hell no Diamond, I want to cum in your wet ass pussy first." She didn't know it was nearly impossible for me to cum while getting my dick sucked. The only person who could do that was Crystal.

Diamond giving me head was marvelous, but I wanted some pussy now. I made her stand straight up and bend over on the cocktail table next to the sofa. She was nearly touching her toes but the table prevented that. I eased all eight inches of my thick and hard dick into her wet pussy as she moaned endlessly. Methodically, I made her place her right knee on the cocktail table and fucked her for a while. Then I asked her to the place her remaining left knee on the cocktail table until she was fully extended. The ambiance of the candles casting a shadow of me going in and out of her from the back continued to turn me on. Diamond was totally screaming by now telling me how good I was stroking her and that she was cumin. Right then, I made her place her shoulders on the cocktail table while she spread her ass cheeks with both hands. On cue, she turned her face to the side so I could view her every emotions. I used my hands to grasp her around the hips as to take any pressure off her shoulders. By now, I was fucking her like a maniac and she loved it. I keep watching her pussy swallow my dick with her thick lips and it stimulated me even more. At one point, I caught myself looking at the Atlanta skyline in front of me while participating in our sex act.

"Take all that dick, Diamond," I shouted while continuing to stroke her. "Give me all that sweet black pussy!"

"Baby, you're fucking me so good please don't stop," she exclaimed. "I'm going to cum again on your hard ass dick."

Before she did I flipped her over onto her back while still on the cocktail table. She didn't miss a beat and fully extended her legs while grabbing both of her ankles. Once again, I eased my hard dick into her now wetter than ever pussy. I stoked her with the beat of the slow music that was playing and passionately kissed her breasts. Then I moved down to her stomach onto her belly button still kissing her gently. All while I still managed to keep my dick in her.

At that point, I wanted Diamond in a new position so I told her to hold onto my neck and get ready for a hell of a ride. She complied and I stood straight up while her legs fitted onto my forearms and I palmed her ass. She was riding me, while I lifted her up and down onto my hard dick. By now we both were yelling like wild hyenas.

After we concluded that position, I maneuvered her back to the sofa and she gave me more head again. While she was giving me head I took a moment to catch my breath and wipe the sweat off my forehead. Then I made her climb on top and ride me right there on the leather sofa. Conversely, she turned around and rode me with her back towards me and her feet on my thighs. It was at this point she came again while she played with her clit.

By now, I was ready to cum and needed to get mine. I figured Diamond was pleased well enough and my job had been done. After she came, I decided I wanted to watch her thick ass shake while I stroked her pussy again. So I made her climb back onto the cocktail table, bent her over and stroked her doggy style until I busted in her. Afterwards and exhausted, we both laid on the large shag run underneath the cocktail table. I held her as she had her back towards me and my dick was still in her. Time had quickly passed as I noticed it was now a little pass midnight and we had been at it for nearly two hours. We took a quick nap right there on the shag rug, then I awoke to her sucking my dick again. All I could do was watch her as the dimly lit candles continued to burn. Before long I was right back up in her, on the rug, in the classic missionary position with her ankles pushed all the way to her ears. This time when I came, I pulled out and aimed straight for her mouth. On cue with her mouth wide open, and tongue extended she clamped down on my dick and swallowed my cum as I moaned with excitement.

Once that was over, Diamond took me by the hand and led me to her bedroom where a king size bed awaited us. There we got under the covers and slept for what seemed to be another few hours, awoke and were at it again. After that, I was out like a light and so was she.

When morning arrived, the sun was beginning to beam through the bedroom blinds as it was almost 7:00 a.m. Diamond's face was turned downwards as I looked over at her. I pulled the covers back to marvel at her thick ass again as she slept on her stomach. The fact that I had my normal usual morning hard on didn't help the situation. Carefully, I kissed her back while she continued to sleep and slowly inserted my erected dick into her. She moaned a little, but her body language was giving the okay to continue. I took this time to simply get a quickie.

After our quickie, I exited her bedroom and found my clothes all over the living room floor mixed with hers. Once my clothes were back on I returned to the bedroom and gave Diamond a kiss on her cheek as she was still in the same position. She told me she would talk to me later and to simply close the front door behind me on the way out as the door would automatically lock.

Walking to the elevator and pleased, I knew I had obtained the number one franchise player on my team. The sex we had was incredible, and Diamond solidified her roster spot. There was no way I'd ever trade her away, well not at least right now.

Chapter 10

It was Saturday morning, and I awoke to a bunch of meddling kids screaming outside my window. As I turned over in the bed, I noticed the time on my clock radio showed 10:00 a.m. Slowly, I managed to roll out of bed and look out my bedroom window through the blinds. Just as I thought, it was an abundance of neighborhood kids playing and making a bunch of noise as usual on Saturday morning. This wasn't a normal Saturday though, it was the Fourth of July, and I guess the neighborhood kids were excited. Looking across the way, I noticed at least three tenants firing up barbeque grills and putting their beer on ice. Quickly, I lay back down in my bed looking aimlessly at the ceiling. I thought to myself how sleep was underrated.

Yesterday, I spent two hours waiting to get a haircut then worked out for another hour at the gym. After the gym, I showered and ran a few errands including paying my rent and utility bills. It seemed as if the day flew by so fast, and there were not enough hours in the day. Suddenly, my cell phone rang and interrupted my thoughts.

"Hello."

"What's up Damien? It's Mookie."

"Happy birthday to you bro," I said. Mookie had a knack for waking up early in the morning no matter what. Even in college he could party all night long but wake up at the crack of dawn with no problem. "What's up with you this morning?"

"Oh, I was just chilling out right now Damien. I got a big night planned with my birthday party and all. Are you still coming out to Club 112 tonight?"

"Yeah, bro, you know I wouldn't miss your party for the world."

"So how did your date with Ms. Booty Shake turn out on Thursday night?" Mookie asked.

"It was the bomb Mookie! She turned out to be the freak I imagined her to be, and the sex was great."

"Did she give you some super head?"

"Hell yeah! You know I wouldn't give her any props if the head wasn't right."

"So where does this chick live?" asked Mookie.

"The Grandview in Buckhead," I replied.

"The Grandview!" shouted Mookie before I could barely get the answer out of my mouth. "Well, you better keep her on your starting five because somebody's got a stash if she lives in that place."

"You know, Mookie, you're the second person that's said that about the Grandview."

"Don't put her on the top of the roster spot yet. You know I got some fine dimes coming through at my birthday party, and they all probably suck a mean dick," exclaimed Mookie. "Hell, I might have to buy me some pussy from one of those strippers tonight."

At that point Mookie and I busted out laughing at that thought. We both knew it was a cardinal sin to buy pussy. No matter if you were in a drought and it was the last thing you did. It was evident especially in Atlanta where the women outnumbered the men ten to one easily. Men who bought pussy were lame cats who had no game but the money they flaunted.

"So Damien, what you got planned for earlier in the day?"

"Just probably relax and watch a baseball game or two before your party kicks off."

"Well you should come over as my mom is having a cookout with all our kin folks coming through," said Mookie. "Plus my uncle is in charge of the grill and he's been known to throw down."

"So what's on the menu for today?" I asked.

"Barbeque chicken and ribs, sausage links, burgers, collard greens, potato salad, candy yams, and macaroni and cheese just to name a few items," responded Mookie.

"How could I refuse Mookie? It all sounds so delicious."

"That's how we get down in the dirty South, Damien." Just come by around two o'clock when all the food should be done."

"Okay bro, I'll see you then."

As I hung the phone up, I realized Diamond had not called me. I brushed it off as she was extremely busy especially with the holidays and all making money. I couldn't be mad at her for getting her paper on. Besides my three day rule was still in effect. Beyond no circumstance should a man call a woman after sex no matter how good it was. Women were emotional creatures and by nature would always follow up with a man after sex. If the woman didn't call you within three days after sex, it was bland or she never had any interest in you anyway.

I finally crawled out of bed and looked at myself in the mirror trying to decide what to wear to Mookie's cookout. After a long thought process I pressed my khaki's Ralph Lauren shorts with my royal blue tee shirt. Then I pulled out my blue and grey '95 Nike Air Max out the closet and placed them next to my outfit. I wanted to dress comfortably as I knew today would be another scorcher with the temperature around one hundred degrees.

I skipped breakfast as I normally did and thought I make up for it with all the food at Mookie's place. Then I shaved and took a hot shower for thirty minutes so my muscles would be relaxed. Afterwards, I put on my clothes, overlook myself in the mirror, and grabbed my car keys headed out the door.

As I was pulling up to Mookie's house there ware cars everywhere. You could definitely tell it was a Fourth of July barbeque. After circling the block a few times, I finally found a parking space and made my way to the house. It was obvious the festivities were in the back yard so I calmly followed a small group making their way to the rear of the house. When I arrived in the rear of the home, I noticed a massive barbeque grill with enough meat on it to feed any army. There was a huge man tending to the grill and I figured it was probably Mookie's uncle. Everyone was so courteous and friendly I had to remind myself it was just southern hospitality.

"Damien is that you?" said a woman's voice as I continued to overlook the scene.

"Hello Ms. Wysinger. "How are you doing?" I asked. It was Mookie's mother who I previously met when I first visited Atlanta. She was a very attractive, dainty, and sweet lady who I had come to respect.

"I'm blessed baby, and how have you been doing?" she asked.

"I'm fine, Ms. Wysinger, and thank you for asking."

"Well, Damien, just make yourself right at home. We have plenty of food, so just help yourself, when you're ready to eat."

"Okay Ms. Wysinger thanks. By the way, where is Mookie?"

"He went into the house for a moment and I'll let him know you're here. But before I do, Damien, there's something I've been meaning to discuss with you."

"Sure, what might that be Ms. Wysinger?"

"Well he's been drinking excessively ever since he came back from college. I think his ego is bruised since the whole baseball thing didn't work out in college. Plus, he has been offered a few menial jobs which don't help. I just want you to look out for my baby tonight, Damien, as he's my only son."

"Say no more, Ms. Wysinger, as you know Mookie is like a brother to me. We both were like two fish out of water when we arrived at the University of Miami. I guess that's why we gelled so well together. I promise I'll look out for him tonight."

"Thank you baby," she said. "Well let me go find Mookie for you, and in the meantime fix yourself something to eat."

"Yes ma'am," I said smiling.

As soon as Ms. Wysinger turned her back, I made a quick dash for the tables where the food was displayed. It was reminiscent of me stealing second base during my glory days at Crenshaw High. The spread was an awesome sight as I was ravaged with hunger by now. I quickly grabbed two paper plates and stockpiled everything I could find. Without being bashful, I figured I could easily work off the extra calories at the gym the next day.

When I finished loading up my plates and looked for a place to sit and eat, Mookie comes barreling out the house. Of course, he already had a drink in his hand celebrating his birthday and barbeque. We gave each other dap as I was careful not to drop my plates full of food. Mookie then pointed to a few empty chairs under and oak tree and we gladly made our way over to the spot. As I devoured my food, Mookie constantly talked about how he planned to have a good time tonight at his birthday party. I pitched the designated driver thought to him as I told him I could do without the alcohol tonight. But Mookie was adamant on driving his mom's Cadillac because he might get lucky. He did promise me that if he did get too tipsy he would pass the car keys. We spend the rest of the evening talking about the old days in college, laughing at what the older guys were wearing at the barbeque, and flirting with some of the women.

By 8:30 p.m., I noticed the barbeque was actually gearing up more. The sun was starting to set but the barbeque, or better yet party, was just getting started. Mookie's mom had hired a well known local dj for the cookout and he was playing all the old school classics from the '70's and '80's. Before I knew it, there was a Soul Train line and everybody young and old joined in. I wasn't too big of a dancer but managed to showcase my grooves when the dj played "Super Freak" by Rick James. The over forty crowd was really beginning to have a ball and they showed it. Even Ms. Wysinger got in on the Soul Train line and shook a leg as I was impressed.

Before long I knew it was time to go as Mookie's birthday party started at 10:00 p.m. but I had to go home, shower, and change my attire. Before I left I thanked Ms. Wysinger for her hospitality and commended Mookie's uncle for the great tasting barbeque. The younger crowd was trickling out as they wanted to hit the nightclubs since it was Saturday night. As for the older crowd they were content with their old school melodies and prepared to dance the night away. As I departed, I gave Mookie dap and told him I would arrive at the club by eleven. Unlike the clubs in Miami, where they closed when the sun came up, the clubs in Atlanta closed right at 2:00 a.m. I figured three hours of partying at Mookie's birthday bash would suffice.

Driving home back to Candler Road, I noticed it was almost nine o'clock now and Diamond still had failed to call me. I checked my cell phone to make sure I didn't overlook any miss calls or voicemails. Then my bruised ego assured me not to call Diamond as I still had one more day to await her call. I assured myself again she was probably busy working with the long holiday weekend.

As I pulled up to my parking space at the apartment complex, the mood was still the same as when I left earlier. Tenants were still grilling and those meddling kids were still running around unattended tearing up what was left of the landscape. Music was blasting from a few units and a couple of teenagers were already popping firecrackers. I assured myself this location was just temporary and as soon as I got a better paying job I was moving out the hood. Besides my college years in Miami, I lived in the hood all my life and I needed a change of scenery. Walking to my apartment, I calculated I had less than a two hour window before departing for the club. I wanted to lie down, relax, and recharge my battery so I could be fresh physically and mentally for the night to come.

Chapter 11

As I pulled up into Club 112's parking lot, I noticed a long line forming with the patrons trying to get in. The clock on my car's console was now showing eleven twenty-one so I figured the holiday drew out the enormous crowd early. As I circled the parking lot trying to find a parking space I couldn't help but notice all the fine and sexy ladies walking up to the club. They all had on scandalous outfits showing their ass and tits. I figured the night would be as close to paradise, and maybe I could add a cutie to my roster. Finally, I managed to find a parking spot close to the club and parked. Mookie told me earlier that I would not have to wait in line tonight. Since he reserved a VIP spot in the club, all his special guests would have the luxury of not waiting in line. Apparently, there was list with my name on it at the front door.

While walking up to the front door of the club, I smiled at a few cuties. They were dressed hot and I had my conservative preppy attire on as usual. I donned as pair of spit shinned Bally loafers with charcoal grey Ralph Lauren slacks. I sported a pinned stripped royal blue Ralph Lauren button down dress shirt to match with a navy blue blazer. My haircut was fresh and styled with pomade to give it that special desirable look. Finally, my belt matched my shoes as always. There was group of guys behind the ladies and one of them yelled out "Where does he think he's going?" Of course, the guys were hatin' because I was going directly to the front door and didn't have to wait in line.

When I arrived at the front door, I told the door man I was there for Mookie's VIP birthday party. He located my name on the list, gave me a quick frisk, and allowed me to enter the club. The club was packed with people already getting their dance on as the dj was playing Master P's "Make Em Say Uhh!" I quickly noticed Mookie's VIP section and made my way to the spot. The VIP section was perfect as it overlooked the entire dance floor.

"What's up Mookie?" I said as I found him relaxing at his table sipping on a cocktail.

"Glad you could make it Damien," he replied as he stood up and we gave each other our customary dap and hug.

"Hey man, sorry I'm late but I had to get an extra nap in after I left your barbeque."

"Don't sweat it, Damien. I just found out the club is not closing until four in the morning. Management told me they extended the hours due to the holiday."

I had already noticed Mookie was slurring his words and by that time he wouldn't have a chance in hell of driving home by himself. As I overlooked the VIP section, there were bottles of Moet, Corona, and mixed drinks on every one of the six tables he had reserved. Mookie and I casually walked over to a few of his homeboys from high school and he introduced me. They were just as ripped as he was, so I figured they too played football at one point in time. He then introduced me to a few females in his VIP section also.

"Okay Mookie, I got you covered if you get too faded. You can always let me drive you home tonight if needed."

"Look bro, I don't want to talk about that right now. I just want to have fun and enjoy my birthday. You need to loosen up anyway. What are you drinking? Better yet, have a shot of Hennessey with me and celebrate."

I reluctantly agreed as Mookie motioned for the waitress then placed an order. I figured we had a long night so maybe one or two drinks wouldn't hurt. The waitress returned with our shots as we grabbed them, made a toast, and turned them up. I felt the alcohol rush through my body and felt a sensation and burning. Within a few moments, I felt like I was on cloud nine and was fully relaxed.

Suddenly, one of the ladies from Mookie's VIP section approached me and started making small talk. Her name was Vanessa and she had all the right curves and a pretty face to go along with it all. Before long we were on the dance floor bumping and grinding as the dj played all the latest hits. As the night progressed, Vanessa and I made our way back over to the VIP section as it seemed like we were on the dance floor for an hour.

Then I noticed three strippers making their way up the VIP section also. You could easily tell they were strippers by their clad dress appearance, makeup, and thickness. Right away they positioned themselves in front of Mookie for a quick discreet performance. They were shaking their asses, touching their toes, and grinding on the birthday boy as he enjoyed himself. Eventually, the strippers calmed down and began to mingle with everybody in the VIP section. Shortly, I noticed Mookie hugged up with one of the strippers while she sat on his lap.

Suddenly, my cell phone began to vibe and I took it off my hip holster to see who was calling me. It was 2:30 a.m. and it was Diamond's number showing on my phone display screen. Quickly, I excused myself from Vanessa and our table as I needed to answer the call.

"Hello."

"Hi baby, its Diamond."

"Well hello stranger. I'm surprised you're calling me so late or even at all."

"First of all Damien let me apologize. I've been meaning to call you but this Fourth of July weekend had me so busy with work and all. It was completely out of my character. I hope you can forgive me?"

"I guess I'll let you slide this time," I said as we both chuckled together.

"Hey, what's all that noise in the background?" Diamond asked.

"I'm at Club 112 celebrating my homeboy's birthday," I replied.

"Really, that's sounds interesting," exclaimed Diamond. "I'm getting off work right now as I decided to call it an early night. The money has been great all weekend."

"So you should stop by over here and see me," I said extending an invitation. "The club doesn't close until 4:00 a.m.

"I think I'll do that, Damien. I'm just right around the corner from you on Piedmont Road. Besides, we can leave the club together and go back to my place so I can give you some much deserved attention."

Right then my dick got on rock hard as I imagined us in hot passionate sex again. I didn't want to seem too anxious for Diamond, but I was craving her sweet black pussy again.

"Okay sweetheart that sounds like a plan. Just let the door man know you're with Mookie's VIP birthday party so you can bypass the line."

"I'm on my way, baby, see you soon!"

And just like that it was on again with Diamond. As I hung up my cell phone I waited a few seconds so my hard on could go down. Then I thought to myself what was I going to do with Vanessa? I figured I'd ditch her with some lame excuse by the time Diamond arrived as I wasn't going to turn down some guaranteed good pussy. Besides I had already exchanged phone numbers with Vanessa and could hook up with her some other time. Before returning to the table where Vanessa was waiting, I made my way to the front door and added Diamond's name to the VIP list.

Within twenty minutes, Diamond had managed to make it to the club, had her car parked in valet, and was walking through the door. Vanessa and I were still sitting in the VIP section as I sipped on a ginger ale trying to figure out what to tell her. She was getting restless, and her body language was telling me she was ready to go home with me but was waiting for me to make a move.

"Hi baby," Diamond said as she walked up to the table where Vanessa and I were seated.

There was Diamond radiant as ever. She had made her way to the VIP section and was turning men and women heads left and right. She stood there in a pair of designer jeans hugging her thick ass but dressed up with a pair of stilettos and a DKNY top. As always her hair was golden blonde, full of body, long, and wavy. Her pretty caramel complexion complimented her million dollar smile.

"Glad to see you sweetheart," I replied as I stood up, hugged, and gave her a kiss on the cheek.

By this time, Vanessa had stood up also waiting for an introduction. Cordially, I introduced the women to each other as they both looked at one another like two angry ex-wives.

"Hello," said Vanessa in an envy mood.

"Hello," replied Diamond in a curt manner. Right then Diamond eyeballed Vanessa as to say "bitch, I'm fucking him tonight."

Seemingly, Vanessa got the picture and excused herself to go mingle with the other people in the VIP section. Before she left, she quietly whispered in my ear she would call me later. At that moment, I offered Diamond a glass of Moet and poured myself one as well. It would be my second and final drink for the night.

"So where's the birthday boy, Mookie?" asked Diamond. "I want to wish him a happy birthday while I'm here."

As I scanned the VIP section, I noticed Mookie a couple of tables over. By now, he was way past drunk and enjoying himself. His stripper friend was still sitting on his lap as he fondled her breasts. I escorted Diamond over to Mookie's table and introduced everyone. By now, I was thinking how was I going to drive Mookie all the way back to Decatur and follow up with Diamond back in Buckhead? I couldn't leave Mookie to tend to himself, nor put pussy before our friendship. Mookie had grabbed me by my arm and pulled me to the side of his table. In the meantime, his lady friend and Diamond got more acquainted.

"Damn Damien, is that the booty shake girl you were telling me about?" Mookie asked.

"Yeah, Mookie, that's her. She wants me to hook up with her again tonight."

"Hell, I'd leave me too if I had somebody as fine as her," remarked Mookie slurring his words.

"Don't even think about it," I said. "You know I'm not going to let you drive all the way back home by yourself. Plus, I promised your mom I would look out for you."

"I got it covered, Damien. My stripper friend, who I've been talking to all night, invited me back to her apartment on Techwood Drive. She rode to the club with her girlfriends and is willing to drive my car."

"What do you know about her, Mookie?"

"Damien, she's cool. All I know is she wants to give me some pussy and I'm not turning that down."

"Alright man, but I'm going to make sure she does drive with no exceptions."

We quickly moved back over to where Diamond and Mookie's lady friend were engaged in a conversation. Diamond gave me the look as if she was ready to go, since she had finished her drink as well. I confirmed with Mookie's friend she was driving and made her take Mookie's keys. Then Diamond and I said our goodbyes to the VIP party and exited the club.

While in front of the club, Diamond gave the valet her ticket as we waited for him to bring her car around. She offered to drive me to my car even though it was only a few yards away. The valet pulled up with Diamond's silver BMW 325i with tinted windows of course. We entered Diamond's car and she drove me over to my vehicle which compared to a clunker next to hers. Before long, I was following her back to the Grandview.

Chapter 12

Shortly after we left Club 112, we arrived at the Grandview. Diamond pulled into the residence's parking area and waited for me to park in the visitor section. After I parked, I jumped into her BMW as we drove up the parking garage to her designated spot. We used the elevator from the parking garage and bypassed the concierge. Before I knew it, Diamond was opening her front door as I anticipated another night of pleasure and fun. As we both walked into her condo, it was still immaculate as before less the lit candles. While standing in front on her leather sofa, she gave me a passionate kiss then abruptly stopped. She pushed me down on the sofa as before and looked at me with a devilish smile. Climbing on top of me, with her clothes still on, we continued to kiss. She gyrated her hips on my dick while I palmed and rubbed her ass. I was on full hard and ready to get undressed when the foreplay stopped.

"Wait baby, I just want to give you a surprise," said Diamond.

"Girl, what kind of surprise do you have for me now?" I asked anxiously. I figured she wanted to grab some whip cream with strawberries or maybe a pair of handcuffs.

"Just follow me Damien." Then she stood up and grabbed my hand leading the way to her bedroom. As we got near her bedroom, I noticed the door was closed but a dim light was transmitting from underneath the door. "Surprise Damien, I hope you like it!" Diamond opened her bedroom door, and there appeared another woman from underneath the covers.

"Damn, Diamond, your ass is a naughty girl," I shouted. "But I like it."

"Damien this is Strawberry. Strawberry this is Damien," replied Diamond as she made the proper introductions. With a name like Strawberry it was obvious she was Diamond's colleague from the Gold Club. But I didn't care as I was all smiles like a five year old on Christmas Day anxious to unwrap his presents.

"So this is, Mr. Damien, with the good dick," said Strawberry. "I heard so much about you. Glad to finally get to meet you as I thought y'all had forgotten all about me."

"Oh no way," Diamond replied. "It just took a minute to get to you, as I had to make a stop, before we made it home."

Instantly, Diamond grabbed Strawberry's hand and pulled her from underneath the covers. Strawberry had a chocolate complexion and was thick and tight from head to toe. Her ass was luscious and her tits were perfectly round. Diamond then grabbed my hand and led us to her master bathroom which was adjacent to her bedroom. On cue, we all three got undressed quickly. Diamond turned the shower on and lit candles keeping the bathroom light off. By now, Strawberry was on her knees with my erect dick in her mouth. Diamond promptly knelled next to her and joined in not letting Strawberry outdo her. They both took turns sharing my dick in their mouth while the other licked my balls.

After they pacified me by sucking my dick on the bathroom floor, I motioned for everyone to enter the oversized shower. The festivities continued and were even better as the hot water drenched over our lustful bodies. While in the shower, I stood back for a while and watched Strawberry and Diamond entertained each other. Soon it was a free for all ménage a trois with everyone pleasing someone in the shower. We were howling like a pack of wild wolves.

By now, I was hot and bothered and wanted to poke both of their pussies with a passion. We all made our way out the shower back into Diamond's bedroom. The hot shower continued to run as the steam matriculated into the bedroom giving off a perfect ambiance.

I quickly lay on the bed with my face up, and Diamond rushed her wet pussy on my dick. She did it so quickly as to let Strawberry know she was getting hers first no matter what. While I stroked my dick into Diamond's pussy and holding her sides she yelled with passion. In the meantime, Strawberry amused herself by licking the base of my dick that wasn't going inside of Diamond. I subsequently took my dick out of Diamond so Strawberry could suck the pussy juice off of it and to keep her in the loop. Diamond then demanded I put myself back in her, and I had no choice but to comply.

Throughout the night, we performed various sex acts as if we were back in L.A. shooting a porno film. Both women had popped a few ecstasy pills earlier and were wet and wild by now. For instance, I would bend Diamond over and fuck her doggy style while she ate out Strawberry and vice versa. In all I came three times that night with the final one shared on the tongues of both women. I lost count how many times they came with or without me, but everyone was fully satisfied. By the time it was all over, the sun was rising as night had gradually turned into morning. I lay there in the king size bed with Diamond on one side of me and Strawberry on the other. Within a few minutes we all fell asleep.

Chapter 13

It was approximately 9:30 a.m. on Monday morning, and I was driving down Candler Road again headed to work as usual. My shift started in fifteen minutes and I wanted to be on time. The Fourth of July holiday flew by so fast, but I was glad I had a blast. I spent all day yesterday trying to recuperate from Mookie's barbeque, birthday bash, and my sexual escapade with Diamond and Strawberry. It was a rarity for me to stay inside all day but yesterday was the exception. I spent all day sleeping and watching nothing on TV while feeling guilty I couldn't make it to the gym.

As I pulled into Macy's employee designated parking spot, Mookie came to mind again. I left him two voice mails yesterday on his cell phone and still had not received a returned call. It was unlike Mookie not to call, but I brush it off that he was still getting over the long weekend as well. Before I exited my vehicle and headed inside the mall my cell phone rang. I noticed it was from an unknown local number.

"Hello."

"Yes, I'm trying to reach Damien Hardy."

"This is Damien Hardy."

"Hello Damien, this is Mr. Richmond from Coca-Cola's Marketing Group. How are you doing?"

"Hello sir. I'm doing well and how are you today?"

"I'm doing well Damien, thanks for asking. I was just returning your call from last week to see if you were still interested in the marketing specialist position with our company?"

"Yes sir, very much so!"

"Well that's great to hear. Are you able to come in for an initial interview this Thursday at 11:00 a.m.?"

"Yes, Mr. Richmond, that fits perfect with my schedule." In reality I didn't know whether or not I was on the schedule to work at Macy's that day but I didn't care. There was no way I was going to miss an interview with Coca-Cola.

"Okay, I'll see you then. Do you know where we are located downtown?"

"Yes, Mr. Richmond, I am familiar with your downtown building location."

"So on the day of your interview just come up the fifteenth floor which is our human resource office. Advise the receptionist you're scheduled for an interview with me."

"Thanks Mr. Richmond that sounds easy enough. I'll see you then."

"See you soon Damien, goodbye."

"Goodbye Mr. Richmond."

Within as few minutes I had managed to secure an interview with Coca-Cola a well known Fortune 500 company. I was elated and figured all my hard work in college was finally paying off. There was no way I could blow the interview or not get the job as I was confident I was the best candidate.

As soon as I hung up the phone with Mr. Richmond, my phone rang again and I noticed it was from another unknown local number. Hesitant, I wondered who was calling me now.

"Hello," I asked thinking was this déjà vu?

"Is this Damien?" said a frantic voice on the other end.

"Yes, this is Damien."

"Damien, thank God I was able to reach you. This is Ms. Wysinger."

"Yes, Ms. Wysinger, what's wrong?" I asked.

My heart sank to my stomach as I knew something terrible had happened. I closed my eyes waiting to hear the worst as there was a long pause before she answered me. The last thing I wanted to do was upset her based on my actions, especially since I had made a promise to her. Finally, after what seemed forever I received a response.

"It's Mookie, he's in the Atlanta City Jail downtown.

"What!" I shouted.

"Damien just listen," pleaded Ms. Wysinger. Please meet me there ASAP. There's been an awful accident, and he's been charged with vehicular homicide!"

Chapter 14

Within seconds after ending the call with Ms. Wysinger, I peeled out of Macy's parking lot like I was at the Daytona 500. There was no way I wasn't going to be supportive for Mookie and his mom in their time of need. As I maneuvered on I-20 westbound headed towards downtown Atlanta, I quickly placed a call to my sales manager from my cell phone to let her know I would be unable to work today. She informed me to handle my personal business and not to worry as today would more than likely be a slow day since the holiday was over. I didn't let her know Mookie was in trouble even though they were relatives as that wasn't my place to solicit anyone's business.

Driving like a speed demon on the interstate, I couldn't help but feel guilty and responsible for what had happened. All I could think about was what went wrong? Did Mookie's lady friend not drive him to her place? How did he get behind the wheel of his car? I kept asking myself these questions trying to seek the answers. Besides that, I felt a sickness to my stomach for what was happening to Mookie. To top it all off, how was I going to face Ms. Wysinger? A few days earlier, I promised I would watch out for her son and now look what had happened.

Finally, I arrived downtown at the Atlanta City Jail and managed to find a public parking spot which charged an outrageous fee. I gave the attendant the required ten dollars and quickly pulled into the space he wanted me to park in. In a hurry, I jumped out of my car but not before placing my parking stub ticket in my front window dash. Then I ran towards the stairs which led to the entrance of the jail's building.

Once inside the jail lobby, I notice how congested it was with people trying to see someone. I quickly viewed the scene trying to find Ms. Wysinger. Within an instant, I saw her sitting down across the way in a sober mood. I could tell she had been crying previously as her eyes were red and swollen. She sat there patiently awaiting my arrival as I took a quick pace to where she was sitting.

"Ms. Wysinger, are you okay?" I asked cautiously.

"Damien I'm so glad you could make it," she replied. She stood up and we both hugged each other.

"First of all, I just want to say I'm so sorry for what has happened," I said in a passionate tone. "Do you know any details of what exactly happened?"

"No Damien, I really don't know what went wrong. I received a call from Mookie this morning, from jail, saying he needed me and wanted you to come too. He then gave me your cell number so I could call you."

"Okay," I said as I continued to listen to her.

"Mookie told me he's already been booked and was being transported to the upstairs unit. Before you arrived, I spoke to a jail administrator who said we could visit with him today for a moment."

"Well that's comforting news Ms. Wysinger. At least we can get to see him and find out what really happened."

We waited patiently in the jail lobby for a few hours as I continued to console Ms. Wysinger letting her know that everything was going to be all right. She even insisted we pray together. After our prayer, she retrieved a small Bible from her purse and read silently to herself. Mookie's mom was the focal point in his life. He had no male figures now or even growing up besides his uncle. So I knew any and all support I could show would be the least I could do.

"Darryl Wysinger," shouted a jailer into the open crowd as he came from behind a large steel door. We knew right then it was our time to visit with Mookie. As we stood up, I raised my hand to let the jailer know we were there to see Mookie. He then motioned for us to approach him, and we followed him to an elevator that led to the eighth floor. Once we got off the elevator, it was obvious we were in a visitation area. The jailer stood by the elevator and pointed for us to walk forward.

"Y'all can go to space number six and the inmate will be with you in a minute," instructed the jailer.

The area was confined and tight as there were designated numbered spaces with a glass partition and a small stool to sit. Besides the stool there was a phone where you could talk to your designated party. There were other individuals already at the other glass partitions, mostly women talking to their male counterparts. We slowly walked forward to the space number six and Ms. Wysinger took a seat on the steel stool while I stood next to her. Then we patiently waited for Mookie to appear.

Mookie finally appeared from the glass partition that separated us. He was wearing an old orange jump suit with flip flops. There was as slight glimpse of worry in his eyes as he approached the stool reaching for the phone. Of course his eyes lit up when he saw his mother and then tears began to fall from her eyes. I knew they needed to be alone for a moment so I backed away to give them their space. Before I left, I made eye contact with Mookie and nodded as to say everything was going to be alright. I then knelt down to Ms. Wysinger and told her I would be near the elevator so she and Mookie could have some privacy. She nodded back in understanding.

While waiting patiently at the elevator, I checked my watch to see how much time had passed. I was surprised twenty minutes had elapsed since we made it upstairs. When I look up from my watch, Ms. Wysinger was approaching me with tears still in her eyes. She told me Mookie wanted to speak with me and she would wait until I was finished. I quickly made my trek down the narrow passage to the number six station and sat on the steel stool while reaching for the phone.

"I'm so sorry Mookie for what has happened," I said as I looked into his eyes.

"It's not your fault Damien why I'm here," replied Mookie.

"But I feel so responsible for what has happened with me promising your mom I would look out for you."

"We all got to hold ourselves accountable for all of our actions in life, Damien. I guess all my bad decisions finally caught up with me."

"Man, what happened that night after I left Club 112?" I asked.

"Well as planned, I hooked up with that stripper and she drove my car to her apartment on Techwood Drive," Mookie said. "After we were at her place for awhile her baby's daddy pulls up starting a commotion."

"So did you have to tussle with him?"

"Hell no as she wasn't even worth that. Plus, he was brandishing heat so I calmly left her spot. While leaving, I hear him slapping and beating her ass."

"What happened next, Mookie?"

"The next thing I knew I was in my ride rounding the Grady curve trying to make it to I-20 towards Decatur. When I looked up there was a Lexus in front of me and everything went black."

"Damn Mookie, why didn't you just call me!"

"I just wasn't thinking Damien. The next thing I know I wake up in the Atlanta City Jail with the jailer telling me I was being booked on vehicular homicide."

"Don't worry Mookie because we are going to do everything in our power to get you out of here. The first objective is to find you a good lawyer and then a bail bondsman."

"Man, I know my bail is going to be steep," exclaimed Mookie.

"Just let us worry about that," I replied. "You just stay focus and keep your head up and we'll be in touch."

"Alright Damien, thanks for everything."

Before we disconnected our call, we gave each other dap on the glass that separated us. Then Mookie was led away by a jailer who took him to his cell. I walked back to the elevator where Ms. Wysinger was sitting in a chair. We hugged again as I continued to let her know Mookie would be fine and everything would work out for the best. As we rode the elevator back down to the lobby, I knew we all were facing a long uphill battle.

Chapter 15

It was 9:30 a.m. on Thursday morning, and the biggest day I had been preparing for had finally arrived. All the countless hours of studying and researching in college were about to pay off. My interview with Coca-Cola was less than two hours away, but I had to mentally prepare myself. As I stood in front of my wall mirror, I figured at least I was dressed for the part. I wore a conservative solid navy blue suit with a pinned stripe dress shirt underneath it. My tie matched my color scheme and was not too flashy. On my feet, I wore a pair of classic black wing tip oxfords which had the business look written all over them. Of course, they were spit shinned to a tee as well.

The drive to downtown Atlanta was no more than twenty minutes away but since the traffic in Atlanta was so unpredictable I decided to leave well in advance. I figured once I got downtown early I could prep myself on the questions Mr. Richmond was going to ask me. Questions like: What are your strengths and weakness? Why do you want to work for Coca-Cola and what was your most challenging situation and how did you handle it? These were basic questions all employers asked potential candidates but you just had to know how to answer them and remain confident.

The last few days had been stressful to say the least. Mookie's accident was still dwelling heavy on my heart and mind. It turned out that the person Mookie struck was a prominent neurosurgeon who was on his way to Grady Hospital to perform a scheduled surgery. To make matters worse, he had a wife, three kids, and was well received in the medical community. The neurosurgeon even had a few books published about his neurological expertise. All this added to Mookie's case which made it political from the beginning. The judge denied Mookie bail due to the severity and his prior DUI cases. By now every news organization in Atlanta was broadcasting the horrific accident involving the neurosurgeon.

Diamond called me right after Ms. Wysinger and I visited Mookie in the city jail. Apparently, she got wind of the event through all the media coverage. She extended her sympathy to both families and told me she was there for me if I needed anything with no questions asked. I saw her sensitive side which I always knew she had, and it made me proud. We even talked about my scheduled interview and she wished me the best of luck. She told me I was the best candidate for the job regardless of the outcome.

Finally, I reached my destination downtown at the Coca-Cola building, and I had a nervous feeling of anxiety. It was now 10:30 a.m., and I had a few minutes to spare. As I anticipated, the traffic on the downtown connector was bottlenecked due to the morning rush hour. I wanted to arrive in the office at least ten minutes before my interview so I could make a good impression on punctuality. After I parked my car in the visitor section of the parking garage for Coca-Coca, I spent a few minutes prepping for my interview. Then I adjusted my tie as I looked in the rear view mirror, grabbed my day planner, and jacket to my suit. As I traveled up the elevator to the fifteenth floor, I put on my jacket and felt a sense of self confident. I felt like a million bucks or at least I thought I looked like it. When I arrived to my destination, the elevator doors opened to a plush lobby area where a receptionist greeted me with a smile.

"Hello my name is Damien Hardy, and I'm scheduled for an interview with Mr. Richmond at eleven o'clock," I said confidently to the receptionist.

"Good morning Mr. Hardy," replied the receptionist smiling at me. "I'll let Mr. Richmond know you have arrived. In the meantime, we just need you to fill out the required paperwork." She handed me a clipboard with a few forms attached.

I gladly accepted the paperwork and took a seat. The paperwork was standard protocol and consisted of an application, background and credit check form, along with a reference check sheet. As I eagerly filled out the forms, I thought maybe some of them were biased a bit. Most black people I knew had tainted backgrounds or bad credit. Maybe the forms were a sophisticated way to weed out minorities in the corporate world, but I had no choice but to comply. At that moment, I couldn't argue with myself as I needed a better paying job right now.

After finishing the paperwork, Mr. Richmond appeared and greeted me in a friendly and professional manner. I gave him a firm handshake and we retreated to his corner office overlooking downtown Atlanta. During the interview process, his questions were predictable as I felt I answered them appropriately and with confident. Once the interview was over, Mr. Richmond thanked me and told me he would be in touch soon. Before leaving, I thanked him for his time and gave him another firm handshake. In all the whole process took about one hour.

The drive back to Decatur was smooth sailing as there was little to no traffic by now. I had to work today but wasn't pressed about getting there. My manager told me to come in once I took care of my personal business the day before. She gave an indication she knew I would be out interviewing for a new job. As I turned off the Candler Road exit, I decided to head in straight to work without changing my attire. By now, I was starving since I had skipped breakfast once again. I figured I would order hot wings from the mall's food court before I clocked in. I was truly addicted to them.

Precisely at nine o'clock, I closed down one of the sales register as I was beat. The day was long and mundane as I could have imagined. After closing the register, I helped my colleagues straighten up a few shoe displays on the sales floor then departed. When I arrived at my apartment a few minutes later, I quickly turned on the shower and began taking my clothes off. Suddenly, my cell phone rang and I noticed it was Vanessa calling me again. She had left a message earlier in the week regarding Mookie, but I was so busy I forgot to return her call.

"Hello," I replied in a tired voice answering my cell phone.

"Hi Damien, its Vanessa. "How are you doing?"

"I'm doing fine Vanessa but just a little tired. I had a long day and I'm just getting off work."

"Well I know you're tired, but I wanted to see if I could come by tonight?" Vanessa asked. "Maybe I can give you a massage to take the tension off of you?"

I knew by the tone in her voice she wanted sex. I thought to myself I wasn't in the mood for any chit-chatting tonight and new pussy would be a great stress reliever. So I figured to cut to the chase and tell her what I wanted.

"Sure you can come by but just be ready when you come through the door," I exclaimed with a sense of arrogance. Then there was a short pause before Vanessa answered.

"Okay Damien, but you better be ready for me as well. What's your apartment number?"

"I'm in C15." I gave her the name of my apartment complex the night we met in Club 112 and apparently she still remembered.

"I'll see you in about fifteen minutes," said Vanessa.

"See you then and don't be late," I replied.

After I hung up the phone with Vanessa, I jumped in the shower and rigorously washed my body from head to toe. The hot boiling water gave me a sense of rejuvenation. When my hot shower ended, I dried myself off and wrapped the towel around my waist. Then I proceeded to brush my teeth and followed up with Scope mouthwash.

Just like clockwork, there was a knock at my door and I knew it could be no one else but Vanessa, especially at this time of night. I walked to the door with the towel still wrapped around my waist. After verifying it was her through the peephole, I opened the door.

Vanessa stood there for a moment smiling and eyeballing my six pack then walked in. She was dressed simple and plain, looking nothing like the person I met in the club. But by now, I really didn't care as her body was still banging. Without hesitation she flung my towel off as I stood there and watched her drop to her knees. My dick sprung on hard quicker than ever and she proceeded to give me head right there.

After about ten minutes of her sucking my dick like a porn star, I grabbed her arm for her to stand up. At first she pulled her arm back in resistance. She was so into sucking my dick and hearing me moan and groan in pleasure it must have been turning her on as well. Then reluctantly, she finally stood up and I led her to my bedroom where she got undressed and we fucked the night away.

Chapter 16

The leaves on the trees were beginning to change colors and fall to the ground as autumn filled the air. Overcast skies showered a gloomy look over the city. It was the second week of October, and I noticed a dramatic change in the weather and scenery. Gone were the luscious foliage and greenery Atlanta was known for. The heat had long since vacated and I was extremely glad of that. Living in Miami for the last five years, I wasn't use to any change in seasons. In Miami, it was eighty degrees or more all year long. People were jogging, riding their bikes, or constantly working out trying to keep their shape. I guess that's why you saw so many beautiful bodies and faces there. In any event, I was looking forward to the change of seasons in Atlanta even if I didn't own a coat.

I managed to secure employment with Coca-Cola and started work right after the Labor Day Holiday. Apparently, they had a grueling background and reference check process that took longer than anticipated. Mr. Richmond even called me back in for a second interview, to meet with upper management, ensuring I was the right candidate for the job. After all that, I gladly accepted the twenty-five thousand dollar a year salary they offered me immediately as a marketing specialist. When Coca-Cola made me the offer, I thought I had hit the big leagues or won the lottery. It was the most amount of money anyone ever offered me. To some my salary could be mediocre but for a twenty-two year old college graduate I was pleased for now. I went from a commission job to a guaranteed paycheck with top tier benefits and I was excited. For a kid coming from South Central L.A. who didn't fall into gangs, drugs, or prison, I thought I did well for myself. My plan was to work hard within the company and with persistence move up the corporate ladder with no problems. Eventually, my salary would increase also.

The crew at Macy's was happy for me landing my dream job in my career field. I even worked out a three week notice instead of the customary two weeks, since my manager was so nice to me. On my final day at Macy's, the staff gave me a farewell surprise cake, balloons, and a card saying they all would miss me. We all exchanged cell phone numbers and promised to stay in touch, but in the end no one ever did.

I even moved out the hood shortly after Coca-Cola made me a job offer in writing. Luckily, I found a quaint apartment near Lenox Road that fitted right into my budget and lifestyle. The location was central to everything in Atlanta, safer, cleaner, and didn't remind me of harsh times in L.A. Even the amenities at my apartment complex were a step up which included a swimming pool, controlled gate access, and washers and dryers within each unit. I definitely felt a sense of accomplishment in my new living arrangement.

Over the last few months, I continued to maintain my sexual relationship with Diamond as she remained the franchise player on my team. She did have a mysterious side that always seemed to peak my interest. It would be days were I couldn't reach or hear from her, then on a whim she would pop up ready to have sex. At this point, I knew it was only platonic between me and her. Plus, she talked about graduating after the spring semester and moving back to Chicago to start her own business. I figured after she left college next year that would be the last I'd ever see of her, so I made the best of the little time we had left.

As for Vanessa, she turned out to be a classic bug-a-boo. She was no comparison to Diamond in the bedroom. The only problem was that she fell in love too early, nagged me to death, and always wanted to know my every move. Every day she would blow up my cell phone as if we were engaged to be married, or ask me where was I. All the attention turned me off as I viewed her as a fatal attraction chick. She even got mad when I moved out of Decatur thinking I was purposely avoiding her. After that,

I had enough and quickly put her on waivers. I stop taking her calls and eventually she got the message. She finally left me alone.

Nicole Jones quickly replaced Vanessa's spot on my roster. Nicole was a thirty-five year old Senior Marketing Manager with Coca-Cola. She had been with the company for the last thirteen years and started right after graduating from college. Despite her age, Nicole had an excellent figure which she managed to maintain by constantly working out. She was married to a man who was vice president of a Fortune 500 Company making over six figures. After her two failed miscarriages, she could no longer have children and this caused her marriage to crumble. Her husband lost interest in her so they simply had a sexless marriage.

I met Nicole during my first day on the job. She was my mentor as I was her protégé. Quickly, she taught me the in and outs of the business and how things operated within Coca-Cola's environment. As we grew to know each other, I became the young vibrant man she was missing in her life and she was the older woman I was always attracted to. Besides that, she was grounded, smart, established, and attractive. These were all the attributes any man would want in a woman. Within two weeks of knowing each other we were intimate. Sexual encounters at her home were the norm as her husband was always on a business trip. She would even book upscale hotel rooms where we would rendezvous during our lunch hour. On one occasion, the sex was so hot during our lunch break, I didn't return back to my desk until two hours had elapsed. Of course, someone snitched to Nicole before the day ended. To rectify the situation, Nicole brought me into her office and gave me a slap on the hand then a blow job.

It really excited me when I was inside Nicole. She came easily and had multiple orgasms over and over again during sex. I couldn't believe her husband was passing that pussy up, but I simply thought his loss was my gain. The perks that came along with Nicole weren't bad either. She made sure I was sharp all the time and showered me with the latest designer clothes and shoes. My car always had a full tank of gas, thanks to her, and my refrigerator was filled with food. To top all that off, Nicole would voluntarily pay my rent and utilities with no questions asked. Now she was making good money working at Coca-Cola but I knew the bulk of my expenses were being paid by her husband's salary. Unfortunately, there was a price to pay for all of these luxuries. Outside of work, Nicole thought we were married as she hung on me tighter than white on rice. At the moment, I was having so much fun I simply enjoyed it for now.

As far as Mookie's situation it went from bad to worst in the last few months. Even though I went to the city jail on weekly visits, his spirit was dejected. He wondered why the accident had happened and what his purpose in life was now. By now, he was truly remorseful and thought the only way to make amends was to go straight to prison. I kept positive thoughts when I was around Mookie so he could keep his head above water. The city district attorney was no help for the situation at hand. He was compelled to offer Mookie's attorney a plea deal of fifteen years due to the public outcry. Of course, Mookie's attorney turned down the deal and both sides decided to head to trial.

Ms. Wysinger remained optimistic throughout the whole process despite the financial and emotional burden she had to bear. She told me her faith in God kept her moving forward knowing there was a plan for what happened to her son. I would often meet with her on Saturdays for brunch and still lend my support. During one of our brunches, she told me it wasn't my fault for what happened to her son. She held no grudges against me. At times, we would even go visit Mookie together if our schedules permitted.

In the end, Mookie's demise was closer than we thought. Even though the city of Atlanta criminal justice system was convoluted and backlogged, they managed to put Mookie's case on the fast track. By the end of summer, of the following year, Mookie was headed to trial. A day before the trial was scheduled to begin; Mookie took a plea deal which gave him ten years in prison. His attorney stated the evidence was too overwhelming for Mookie to prevail at trail. Before being sent to prison, Mookie told me he wouldn't allow anyone to see him in the penitentiary except his mother. I had no choice but to respect his wishes. After that, we communicated by phone calls and letters only.

I learned one thing through Mookie's ordeal and that was life was too short to be taken for granted. The world doesn't stop for anyone or events that occur. We chalk up a loss and somehow have to find a way to move forward in life as everyone does. As Mookie would have wanted it, I had to find a way to move on. Ms. Wysinger, despite her loss, would not have to question God's chosen path for her son. Above all, Mookie would have to endure his confinement and rebound from it all. He would have our help, support, and love along the way.

Part IV

Full Circle

Summer 2008: Atlanta, Georgia

Chapter 17

It was Friday, June 13th and a normal work day at Coca-Cola, well at least what I thought. The last ten years at Coca-Cola went on without a hitch. My work product never slacked and my yearly salary continued to increase. Over the years, I managed to work myself up the corporate ladder from an entry level marketing specialist to a senior marketing analyst. By now, I was responsible for ensuring all marketing documents and presentations were precise. They had no legal flaws before they were submitted to various clients. It was a step up from my first position where I handled sales calls and tired to solicit Coca-Cola's business to potential million dollar clients.

My relationship with Nicole was still vibrant as ever, even though you would have thought it would have fizzled out by now. She was promoted to marketing director making six figures with a corner office but her personal life was still in shambles. Her sexless marriage was over long ago but she still cohabitated with her husband less the sex. I figured Nicole didn't want to be all dressed up with nowhere to go since she was now forty-five years old. A successful business woman without a husband could have been taboo in her eyes. So she dealt with all the nonsense between them both and remained married. Besides, she had invested too much time and money into the marriage and leaving now just wasn't an option. I often asked myself, how could someone be married and miserable? For now, I was happily single and loving every minute of it.

At approximately 2:00 p.m., I was sitting down in my chair preparing to finish up some work before the day ended. A colleague and I went to the Varsity for our normal Friday afternoon lunch an hour earlier. Taking a late lunch was always better to help avoid the midday rush and it made the afternoon pass quicker. As I attempted to log back on my computer, I received an error message which read: incorrect password. "Incorrect password," I shouted to myself while looking at my computer. Then I proceeded to retype my password and slowly this time. The computer system relayed the same message as I thought something must be wrong with the system. We all had system generated computers that automatically told us when it was time to change our passwords. Since it was not near the normal ninety day window, I was confused by now. Once again, I prepared to enter my password into the system and typed it super slow: D-O-D-G-E-R-S-1-2-3. Finally, the system responded with the same incorrect password message. "What the hell is going on here," I said in a heated voice while looking around at my co-workers.

Suddenly, I received an email alert on my BlackBerry letting me know I had an incoming message. I had my work email synced to my BlackBerry so I wouldn't miss any important communications with upper management or my clients. As I retrieved my BlackBerry from my waist holster, I quickly read the message which stated for me to report to Mr. Richmond's office at once. Mr. Richmond still worked in human resources and had sent the message himself. A sense of anxiety rushed through me as I wondered what Mr. Richmond would want from me. Quickly, I shifted out of my seat and rose to my feet headed towards the elevator. A few of my co-workers glared at me then shifted their eyes back to their computer screens. When I boarded the elevator headed down to the fifteenth floor I replayed the last few weeks at work over in my mind wondering if I did something wrong. Finally, the elevator doors opened as I had reached my destination. Mr. Richmond's office was still plush as it was ten years ago on my first interview but the furniture and pictures had been changed. Although the receptionist was different, she still was young, polite, and friendly.

"Hello, I'm here to see Mr. Richmond," I said to the receptionist approaching her with hesitation. It was like déjà vu all over again as I thought about my first interview.

"Hi, Mr. Hardy, Mr. Richmond is expecting you," replied the receptionist with a smile. "You can simply go back to his office now."

As I made my way down to Mr. Richmond's office, my nerves were on edge with knots in my stomach. When I arrived, Mr. Richmond was sitting at his desk with his back towards the open door as he looked out the large windows at the Atlanta skyline.

"Mr. Richmond, it's Damien," I announced while knocking on his door at the same time.

"Ah, Damien, please come in and close the door behind you," he replied as he turned around to face me. "Would you like to sit down?"

"Sure," I said as I reluctantly sat down in a cozy chair in front of his desk.

"Well Damien, I'm going to get right to the point. You know we're in an economic turmoil right now. The housing and financial markets have crashed and Coca-Cola isn't making a lot of money right now."

"Yes, Mr. Richmond, I watch CNN so I am aware of what's going on with the economy."

"Damien, what I am trying to say is somewhat difficult. We came to a consensus decision within the company to scale back on certain departments. Thus, regrettably were going to have to terminate your position effective immediately."

"What!" I shouted at the top of my voice. "My record here is impeccable and every year I exceeded expectations. Why is the company letting me go?"

"I know you've been an exceptional worker," said Mr. Richmond with a straight face. "But right now, it's about budget constraints and all departments will be affected."

"I gave this company ten years of hard work and dedication and this is how I'm rewarded," I exclaimed as I was way pass hot by now.

"Believe me, Damien, it was not my decision as it came from upper management," he replied in a cavalier tone. "We will gladly pay you one month's severance, and then you'll be able to file for unemployment benefits."

I stood there speechless looking at Mr. Richmond like my whole life had ended. I could not phantom ever leaving Coca-Cola and now I had been terminated by the company I gave so much too. I thought about all the countless hours that manifested into years working for the company and now it was all for nothing. Irately, I turned around and stomped towards Mr. Richmond's office door. When I opened the door, there were two company security officers waiting on me. I was told by one of the security officers my personal items, on my desk, would be mailed to me and all my access to the building was now denied. The two security officers advised me they would have to escort me to the first floor of the building.

I felt like a prisoner. I was escorted to the elevators and noticed the receptionist shifting papers, on her desk, as if she didn't know what was going on. She even avoided eye contact with me. When we arrived on the first floor, I gave my access building card to the security officer per his request and quietly exited the building never looking back. Just like that, my career with Coca-Cola was over as my pride took a nosedive.

Once I walked over to my black BMW 745i I quickly jumped into it for some added security still amazed at what just happened. I peeled out of the parking deck and made my way into the early Friday afternoon rush hour traffic. Suddenly, my BlackBerry began to vibe as I maneuvered angrily into traffic. "Now who could be calling me?" I said aloud retrieving the phone from my waist holster. Surprisingly, it was Nicole's number showing on my phone display.

"Nicole, you're not going to believe what just happen to me," I stated while answering the phone.

"Damien, I already know," she replied in a soft tone before I could almost finish my sentence. "I'm so sorry it had to happen to you."

"Huh? I know wildfires spread quickly but you couldn't have heard about me that fast. Did you already know I was being terminated today?"

"Yes dear, the executives told me two weeks ago as you were staffed under my department."

"What the hell!" I said frantically. So you had the audacity not to tell me I was being terminated?"

"Baby please you don't understand," she said trying to smooth things over. "I was sworn not to tell under confidentiality by Coca-Cola. If word got out my job would have been in jeopardy."

"Forget you Nicole!" I said with a passion. At that moment, I couldn't believe how a woman I trusted for the last ten years could keep my termination from me.

"Damien, you just don't know what I've been going through as well," said Nicole. "Maurice lost his job last month due to the recession and things have been difficult for us financially and emotionally."

"Damn it, Nicole, stop complaining about your tired ass husband to me! I'm in no mood to hear about your melodrama marriage today."

"Damien, I know you're upset and disappointed and that's why I reserved a suite for us at the Ritz-Carlton for the next two days. We can unwind with a nice candlelit gourmet dinner."

"No thanks, Nicole, I think you just don't get it," I exclaimed.

I wasn't in the mood to deal with her or pacify her sexual appetite for the moment. Rudely, I hung up the phone and tossed my BlackBerry over my shoulder into the back seat continuing to drive through downtown Atlanta.

Chapter 18

It was the following Monday morning as I awoke looking at my alarm clock which read seven o'clock. My internal clock always woke me up early every weekday morning so I could make it to work by 8:30 a.m. As I position my body to get out of bed, I realized I had nowhere to go today. Then I lay back in the bed while staring at the ceiling fan continuously turning. There was a constant red light on my BlackBerry which meant voicemails and text messages were waiting. I figured my former colleagues and Nicole was trying to reach me all weekend. As far as I was concern, they all were part of my past now.

Within the next hour, I was up and in my condo fixing myself a bowl of Frosted Flakes for breakfast. Before stretching out on my leather recliner, I opened the blinds so the mood wouldn't be so depressing. As the sunlight trickled in, I could hear the hustle and bustle of traffic as people made their way to work for the day. I decided to listen to one of the R&B music video channels on TV. All the major networks were discussing the plight of the U.S. economy including more banks folding and home foreclosure rates increasing. To make matters worse, the unemployment numbers were so alarming and now I was a casualty of the same. When a Sade video came on it set the morning mood right and I was able to begin eating my bowl of cereal. Cereal was one constant in my life that would never change.

Ever since I was a kid I loved Frosted Flakes and they never grew old to me.

After finishing my bowl of cereal, I sat there listening and watching videos contemplating what I would do with my life now. Trying to find a job in this economy was nearly impossible. I thought about calling up Nicole and giving into her sexual innuendos so she could put me back on her payroll. But the more I thought about it the more it left a sour taste in my mouth. Nicole wasn't living up to her billing spot on the roster and that spark between us was damn nearly burnt out. All she talked about lately was her husband and broken marriage. I was feeling more like her therapist rather than her fling.

As I made my way to the sink, placing the empty cereal bowl into it, I decided I might as well go work out today and blow off some stress. The last thing I was going to do was let my body get fat and flabby which I could never forgive myself for. Every day at work I saw guys with pot bellies and convinced myself that would never be me. To make matters worse, these guys were no older than me. What a bunch of lazy bums, I always thought to myself. I'd only managed to put on a few pounds since graduating from college and still had my muscular physique. I owed it all to a proper work out regiment of at least four days a week and a well balanced diet. A good thirty-five minute jog on the treadmill while I listen to my iPod always seemed to help me blow off stress. Of course, my iPod always had a vast collection of Tupac's greatest hits to keep me in the workout mood. Then I would follow that up with another twenty-five minutes of strength conditioning by lifting weights.

After quickly changing into my workout attire and headed to the gym for a workout, my BlackBerry rang. I had avoided answering all phone calls for the weekend or check messages including texts. As I picked my phone up, I noticed whoever was calling me had a private number which always annoyed me. I contemplated on whether or not to answer the call wondering who was calling me from a private number. Maybe it was pestering Nicole still trying to reach me or my former colleagues. I didn't want to be bother with either one right now, but I went ahead and answered the call reluctantly.

"Hello," I said in a low tone voice.

"What's up, Casanova? This is Mookie."

"Hey how's everything with you Mookie? I asked. "It's been a moment since I last heard from you."

It had been roughly six months since I last received a call from Mookie. Most of the time he would call me from a cell phone that someone else figured out how to smuggle into the prison. He rarely called me from the pay phones in the facility or wrote me letters as he said the prison monitored them too intensively. Most of Mookie's phone calls were sporadic at best and I never knew when he would reach out to me.

"Everything is great bro," replied Mookie. "I'm actually being released next week on time served and wanted you to come pick me up."

"Say no more, partner," I said with excitement. "You know I have no problem of coming to pick you up. Just let me know the date and time."

"Yeah Damien, I really appreciate that but I'll call you in a day or so with the specifics. Got to go man, cause I think I hear a CO coming making his rounds. Peace bro."

"Peace, Mookie."

After I hung up the phone with Mookie, I couldn't actually believe what had happened. Mookie was finally getting out of prison after ten long years. The time passed fast as the accident seemed so long ago. But I knew for Mookie the last ten years were probably slow and crucial, especially not having your freedom and all the luxuries people take for granted. The sluggish economy wasn't going to be good news for an ex-offender, but I was sure Mookie would prevail through it all as he did in the past. He still had me, his mom, and uncle as a great support system. We all knew Mookie was a "survivor". If he made it through prison he could make it though anything now. With the biggest smile on my face in a long time, I grabbed my Gatorade and towel then headed to the gym.

By the following Wednesday, I was headed to Hancock State Prison to pick up Mookie who was scheduled to be released at 11:00 a.m. The drive to the prison was two hours east of Atlanta, but I got an early jump on the day. The night before I couldn't sleep too well and was filled with nervousness waiting to see my friend again. I wondered how he would look and what was the first thing he would want to do? By eight o'clock, I was on I-20 eastbound going against the flow of rush hour traffic. The last thing I wanted to do was be late, so I departed well in advance. Before I left, I invited Ms. Wysinger to ride with me but she declined. She told me she didn't want to see the menacing prison walls again. Plus, she wanted me and Mookie to catch up on some conversation as we drove back to Atlanta. Ms. Wysinger had prepared a welcome home greeting for her son, which included a cake, balloons, and his favorite meal. She anticipated seeing him walk through her door and giving him a long hug with a motherly kiss.

As expected, I arrived in Sparta, Georgia, shortly after 10:00 a.m. The town was a small community and you could miss it if you blinked twice. Thank God I had a navigation system in my car, otherwise I would have easily gotten lost. Being from L.A., traveling in the rural South was not one of my strong points. When I got closer to the prison, I noticed the menacing prison wall Ms. Wysinger had mentioned to me. It had to be at least thirty feet high and had barbed wire on top of it as it surrounded the entire prison. I quickly located a sign pointing to visitor inmate reception and pulled my clean BMW into the area. As I exited my car, I noticed there were surveillance cameras everywhere. When I walked up to the entrance door there was a call box with a white button that I pushed.

"Yes sir, how may I help you?" said a sexy female's voice from the call box.

"I'm here to pick up Darryl Wysinger," I said nervously. "He's being released today."

Suddenly, there was a loud buzz and the huge steel door was opened for me to enter into the facility. As I walked in, there stood a male guard who had me sign in, empty my pockets into a plastic bowl, and searched me with a hand held metal detector. Then the guard placed the plastic bowl with my contents on a conveyor belt which ran through an x-ray machine similar to the ones at the airport. Next the guard motioned for me to walk through another metal detector where I ended up in a waiting area.

"Sir, you can just have a seat here in the waiting area," said the guard in a real country accent. "Mr. Wysinger is still being processed for release and will be out directly."

I replied with a simply "okay" and took my contents from the plastic bowl while taking a seat. By now there was another visitor being buzzed in and the guard walked back towards the steel door. As I sat there patiently, I noticed there wasn't a clock on the wall so I looked down to my watch on my wrist. It was now twenty minutes till eleven and hopefully Mookie would be approaching soon. The visitor area floor was sparking clean as a trustee slowly went back and forth over it with a large dust mop. The trustee had to be at least sixty years old as grey hairs filled his entire head. He never made eye contact with me but continued to work a slow routine.

By eleven o'clock, as promised, Mookie was walking through another steel door near the waiting area. As the door opened up, there was Mookie grinning from ear to ear and carrying a large box full on items he collected over the last ten years. I stood and smiled back waiting for Mookie to approach me. Once he got closer I wrapped my arms around his neck and hugged him with joy as he still clung onto the large box. He finally dropped the box and we both hugged each other as if we were real brothers. From what I could tell he was still built like a NFL linebacker but with a few added pounds.

"Man, I'm glad to finally get to see you again Damien."

"I'm glad to see you also Mookie and it's great to know you're finally getting out of this place."

As Mookie picked up his box of contents we made our way to an exit door. Before we left, an older guard came up and gave Mookie a firm handshake wishing him the best of luck. Even the trustee worker reappeared and said his final farewell to Mookie. When we got outside the exit door, Mookie instantly fell to his knees and kissed the ground. The he looked upwards towards the clear sky and thanked God for his freedom. All I could do was smile and be thankful as well. When Mookie got off his knees we gave each other dap and a hug again. Then we made our way over to my car and I took Mookie's box from him.

"I see you did well, Casanova," exclaimed Mookie. "That seven series bimmer is hot! Your tint and chrome wheels really set it off."

"Thanks Mookie," I said. "I see you still remembered my dream car."

"How could I forget," Mookie said. "It was all you talked about when we were in college."

We both laughed as we prepared to enter my vehicle. I placed Mookie's box in the truck as we positioned ourselves for the drive back to Atlanta. As I pulled out of the prison facility, I noticed Mookie simply looking forward. He had no intentions of looking back at the prison or what it resembled. Within a few minutes we were out of the rural area and back on I-20 headed towards civilization.

Over the next two hours, Mookie and I laughed and caught up on old times. We talked about our college days and when I first moved to Atlanta. We even laughed at his "starting five doctrine" that Mookie educated me on while we were at the University of Miami.

I showed Mookie my BlackBerry and how far cell phone technology had advanced in the last ten years. He fumbled around with the device but it was really Greek to him at first. Then he figured out how to use it and even called his mom letting her know we were on the way home. Mookie told me in prison resources to keep up with the free world were limited but they managed the best they could.

During many of our conversations, Mookie asked about Diamond and I told him I never heard anything else from her after she graduated from Spelman College. Apparently, she moved back to Chicago for a brighter future. I even broke down and told Mookie what had happened to me at Coca-Cola. He optimistically responded that things happen for a reason, and the only way to be in economic control of your future was to be your own boss or entrepreneur. That piece of information seemed to have stuck out the most during our ride back to Atlanta.

By early afternoon, we had made it back to into the suburbs of Atlanta headed towards Mookie's mom house in Decatur. As we drove through Conyers, he was amazed how the area had grown from a former farm area not so long ago. Then when we past Stone Crest Mall in Lithonia, all he could do was gawk at how much the area had changed.

Finally, we pulled up into Mookie's mom driveway and noticed the balloons and decorations on the outside of the house. While I was retrieving Mookie's box from my truck, he ran into his mother's house with excitement. Once inside his mom gave him the most deserved hug ever which seemed to have lasted forever. Ms. Wysinger began to cry with joy and I even felt tears developing in my eyes. Even Mookie's uncle was there to greet and welcome him home. The "Welcome Home Mookie" banner filled the living room along with red and blue balloons. We could smell the aroma of Ms. Wysinger's southern cooking which included fried chicken, macaroni and cheese, collard greens and candy yams. She even cooked a red velvet cake which was Mookie's favorite.

We spent the rest of the day celebrating, feasting, and revisiting good memories from the past. It was a joyous time for all of us. We could finally put the negative past behind us all and look towards a brighter future now that Mookie was home for good.

Chapter 19

It was almost two weeks since I had picked up Mookie from prison. How ironic that the Fourth of July weekend had crept upon us again and everyone wanted to celebrate. First, Mookie would celebrate his thirty-third birthday outside of the prison walls with his family and friends. Secondly, Mookie's birthday and the Fourth of July holiday were being celebrated on the same day. It was Saturday, July 5th and Ms. Wysinger had extended an invite to everyone to celebrate at her home. Once again, Mookie's uncle was in charge of the barbeque grill. Of course, Ms. Wysinger prepared the traditional holiday meal including macaroni and cheese, collard greens, pasta salad, barbeque baked beans, and potato salad.

I had arrived early for the barbeque well in advance for the late afternoon start. I figured I could help the family with food preparations or anything else I could fit in. It wasn't as if I needed to go work that day. I had been out of work for almost a month now and I was still trying to get adjusted to my current situation.

Later that evening, the barbeque celebration was in full swing. All the guests had arrived with everybody stuffing their faces with the great food including myself. As before, there was a dj playing all the latest hits from the 70's, 80's and early 90's. It was the way Ms. Wysinger wanted it. She told me long ago that old school music was full of soul and had a message and meaning. Unlike the new era of rap music which had drastically changed since I grew up, I couldn't do more but agree with her on that point.

I took it upon myself to have a few extra beers that hot day to help me alleviate the stress I was going trough without a job. As I stood there with a bottle of Heineken in hand, I noticed Mookie didn't have anything to drink all day. He was simply enjoying himself without the alcohol. As soon as he saw me relaxing with a brew, he approached me wanting to talk.

"So how have you been doing Damien with your job search?"

"Man it's crazy out here, Mookie. Everywhere I look companies are shutting down their doors and laying off workers. I just try to remain confident and continue to network."

"Yeah, I know too. It's especially hard for a brother who just got out of the penitentiary. So you ever give any additional thought about being your own boss?" Mookie asked.

"Not really," I replied. "I guess now would be the perfect time since the country is in a major recession."

"You ever thought about a part time hustle that caters to women," said Mookie. "It's practically foolproof, being that woman love to shop."

"I know you're not up to a no good scheme," I exclaimed. "You just got out the joint."

"Damien, all I'm saying is that woman love to shop. They spend their last on clothes, shoes, and purses."

"Tell me something I don't already know Mookie."

"Well while I was in the penitentiary, I befriended a guy who was serving time for a fencing racket," Mookie started explaining. "He has a connection to all the major designer outfitters and he was released six months before me."

"I don't know Mookie, sounds a little shady to me. Besides where is this connection getting his product from?"

"Some of it is fenced goods taken from warehouses or loading docks before it makes it to the high end retailers," said Mookie. Other products are simply knockoffs imported from China. You pick your products, pay wholesale and sale for retail."

"So where do you sell these items?" I asked.

"Any and everywhere" Mookie replied. "Salons, purse parties, and even direct to those corporate chicks you once worked with. I'm telling you bro, you can make a killing in tax-free dollars."

And just like that Mookie had turned me on to a new hustle that seemed pretty straight forward with a lot of financial incentives. I initially worked in sales when I first started working at Coca-Cola and felt I could sell anything to a prospective buyer, especially woman.

"If you're interested, I'll give you more details in a couple of days Damien. I'm supposed to meet with my connection to view the products. You can simply buy your products through me."

We spent the rest of the night partying and having fun. I never saw Mookie take a drink as he continued to enjoy himself. I figured Mookie had made a conscience decision he could now have fun without the alcohol.

Chapter 20

By now my severance pay with Coca-Cola had ended and I was compelled to file for unemployment benefits. Today was Thursday morning, and I decided to go to the Georgia Department of Labor to initiate my benefits. There was an office on North Druid Hills Road which was near my Buckhead condo which made it convenient for me. I dreaded having to deal with the long lines and bureaucratic paperwork that comes along with most government agencies. At this moment in time, I really didn't have any other option as my only other source of income was exhausted. My weekly unemployment benefits amount would be a mere pittance of what I was accustomed to making but for now it was some form of income.

When I arrived at the Georgia Department of Labor, it was crowded as expected. The line for unemployment benefits was long and probably contained at least thirty-five people ahead of me. There were long and gloomy faces on just about everyone in the line. I quickly assumed my position in the line and waited for someone to assist me. As I looked around, while waiting in line, I noticed there were individuals sitting in chairs holding number slips waiting to be called as well. After what seemed about an hour, I finally made it to the front of the line where a calm gentleman asked how he could help me. I told him about my company terminating me and showed him my separation letter. After he reviewed my letter, he punched my social security number into the computer he was sitting behind. I was then given a number and told someone would call out my name for an orientation class. I then proceeded to take a seat in the waiting area where everyone else was sitting.

Nearly another hour had passed when a small petite woman walked up advising everyone orientation was beginning. She called out a group of numbers and directed everyone to follow her. My number was called out nearly last as I was thankful I didn't have to wait for another orientation to begin. Like a head of cattle, we all followed the woman to a conference room in the back of the building. The orientation was remedial, at best, as we were given basic instructions on who was entitled to benefits and how to file the same. After that process was over everyone in the group were directed to a computer to fill out an application and certify for benefits. By the time that process was over I was free to leave and told I would receive an award letter in the mail.

After spending more than half a day applying for unemployment benefits, I decided to hit the gym for a well deserved workout. When I arrived back at my condo, I quickly changed into my workout attire, grabbed a lemon lime Gatorade out the frig, and headed out the door once again. The gym was located on the second floor in the condominium building where I lived. This made it extremely easy for me to get a workout in whenever I wanted. Plus, the gym was always open twenty-four hours per day.

When my intense workout was over I took the stairs back up to my condo located on the twelfth floor. I always took the stairs after my workouts as I felt guilty if I took the elevator. Once I reached my condo, I took my normal twenty minute boiling hot shower to help relax my throbbing muscles and stressful mind. When my shower was completed, I threw on a pair of fleece Adidas jogging pants and a grey tee shirt hoping to relax for the rest of the day. I immersed myself on my leather sofa and turned the TV on to the jazz music channel and closed my eyes. Within a few minutes my late afternoon nap was disturbed by a loud knock on my front door. At first I thought I was dreaming but then I realized I wasn't when I opened my eyes.

"Bang, bang, bang, bang, bang," was the sound coming from my front door. "Damien open the door, it's me Nicole. I know you are in there because I saw your car in the parking garage."

I rolled my eyes and shook my head thinking why the hell Nicole is being so persistent as ever. It had been over a month since we had a conversation or sex and I thought she had gone on with her life.

"Damien, please open the door," screamed Nicole as she continued to bang louder on my door. "I just came by to check on you and make sure you're alright."

As I sat upright on my sofa, contemplating whether or not to open the door I took a deep breath. Then I figured I had nothing to lose. This would be a good time to tell Nicole about my potential new hustle and she could turn me on to her corporate girlfriends for sales. I rushed to the door and looked through the eyehole making sure it was her. Just as I imagined, she stood there in her conservative blue business dress attire holding what seemed to be a takeout box of food. Brothers don't turn down food, too often, so I gladly opened the door.

"You think you're going to get rid of me that easy since you don't work at Coca-Cola anymore?" asked Nicole as we both made eye contact. She quickly made her way into my condo so I couldn't shut the door in her face after that smart comment.

"Well hello to you too," I replied sarcastically. I thought to myself Nicole must be one lonely woman or a psychopath, as I took a glimpse of her ass in the tight skirt she was wearing. Then I finally closed the front door.

"Damien, I brought you a plate from Justin's," exclaimed Nicole as she sat down on my leather sofa placing the takeout box on the cocktail table. "It's your favorite: half baked chicken smothered in mushroom gravy, collard greens, steamed rice, and a sweet roll."

"So where's the dessert," I asked. "You know I love their chocolate cake." By now we were both sitting on the sofa in a relaxed manner.

"I'm your dessert baby!" exclaimed Nicole in a crazy glare at me. "You want to eat me…um I mean eat your dessert first? Besides I took the rest of the day off just to be with you."

I knew right then from her devilish grin Nicole wanted to give me some and that her pussy would always be mine no matter what transpired between us. So I sat back and let her have her take at me. Nicole ripped off my fleece jogging pants like an eager child at a birthday party. Then I helped her finish unwrap the package by pulling off my shirt. She caressed her soft hands over my chest then my rock hard abs. Slowly, she kissed me on my belly button then quickly put me into her mouth. My rock hard dick gladly awaited her thick lips and warm soothing tongue. Up and down she stroked me with no hands showing off while watching me with her eyes. I had no choice but to moan in pleasure as I had forgotten how great she was at giving head.

"I'm so sorry, Damien," she said softly while briefly taking me out of her mouth. Then she continued to massage my dick with her hand and licked my balls.

After I groaned for a while watching her deep throat me, I wanted to enter her with a passion. She knew that always got me over the top when she did that. But I knew our foreplay moment weren't quite over yet. I made Nicole strip naked for me to the soft jazz tunes from the TV channel. While she stripped she made sexual gestures like holding her breasts, licking her nipples, and moaning at the same time. Then she even teased me more by taking off her thong, spreading eagle on the floor while she lay on her back and played with her clitoris.

"I know you want some of this sweet black pussy, Damien," Nicole said while still playing with herself on the floor. "You know my pussy is so tight since you haven't been in it. Daddy missed mama while I've been away?

Nicole had me hotter than ever and she knew it as I watch her from the sofa. Before I entered her I wanted to please her too. I made her get off the floor and join me back on the sofa in the sixty-nine position. While she licked my dick I sucked the hell out her wet pussy spanking her as she shook her thick ass in my face. The ass slap turned her on even more as she continued to suck me off trying to get me to explode in her mouth.

"You gonna be a good girl and not hold anything else from daddy," I shouted as a slapped Nicole's ass repeatedly.

"Ooooh! Yes daddy I promise I'll be a damn good girl from now on," she replied just long enough to answer then placed my dick back into her mouth.

But I knew I had to really punish her for being such a naughty girl. The only way she would learn was by anal fucking her. Nicole was into all kind of kinky shit and anal was her favorite on special occasions. We didn't do this all the time just to break the monotony of regular sex and when I needed to make a point. I made her rise off my head and positioned her doggy style on the sofa. Her shoulders were paralleled to the sofa and her ass was tucked all the way up. Right then, I ran to my bedroom and retrieved the KY jelly from my nightstand. When I arrived back to Nicole she was still there spread out and toying with me by shaking her ass from left to right. I lather my hard dick and proceeded to enter her. She helped me out by reaching back with a hand and spreading her ass cheek. As my head poked into her asshole she yelled with pleasure telling me to continue. With slow steady strokes my eight inches was fully inside her ass.

"Now let your ass cheek go and play with your pussy clit," I said to her.

"Oh Damien I missed that thick dick of yours," she screamed. "You feel so good inside my ass, baby."

I continued to stroke her asshole harder and harder as she continue to yell in pain. Her yells did nothing but turn me on even more knowing I was fully in charge. We both knew how to stimulate each other so well we came together. As I exploded into her anal cavity she maneuvered her ass back and forth on my dick while she came stimulating herself. Then we got off the sofa and I carried her into my bedroom for more comfort.

"Thank you Damien, I needed that," she said as we lay in the bed holding each other.

"Yeah, that was the bomb," I replied basking in the moment.

Within a few moments, Nicole began massaging my balls claiming she wanted her pussy stroked now. Eagerly, I complied with her wishes and made her get on top. During the rodeo show, I watched the action in my dressers' mirror which was positioned in front of the bed. Afterwards, I made her ride me with her feet flat of the bed so my dick could fully extend into her. When she did this I used my fingers and played in her asshole stimulating her even more. Her slow strokes turned steady, then fast ones as she rode me. Then as always, I climaxed and she did the same shortly thereafter.

When we both woke up later the evening haze was developing over the Atlanta skyline. The hot passionate sex had tired us out but the nap revived us. Nicole look at her watch as it was the only thing she was wearing.

"Damien, I got to go as it getting late. It's already six-thirty and Maurice will be expecting me home soon to cook dinner."

"Well, you better jump your ass in the shower and wash that sex scent off of you."

"I know, right. Are the towels in the same place?" Nicole asked. "What about my spare toothbrush? I know you didn't throw it away."

"As always, you know nothing ever changes over her," I said. We both looked at each other and began to giggle.

Nicole jumped out of my bed and made a run for the bathroom so she could take a steamy hot shower. I threw on a pair of boxers and decided to join her in the bathroom. At this point, I could tell her about my hustle.

"So Nicole, what type of designer purses and shoes are hot with women now?"

"Did you say designer purses and shoes, Damien?" She quickly peeked out from behind the shower curtain.

"Yeah, you heard me right. What's hot with the ladies now?"

"Well, I specifically like Jimmy Choo and Christian Louboutin. Why do you ask?"

"I might have the hookup on designer purses and shoes," I said. "My partner has a connection with some people who have high end merchandise. I thought maybe I could sell these items and supplement my near to nothing income right now."

"Damn Damien that's sounds like a good idea," remarked Nicole. "It's a bit risky but still a good idea. I can put you in touch with all my girlfriends who love to shop."

"Any idea on how I can showcase the products to your girlfriends?" I asked.

"Well for one, we can have a purse and shoe party at one of my girlfriend's house," she said. "We can even add hors d'oeuvres and cocktails while the ladies mingle and shop your displays."

"That sounds like a great idea, Nicole."

"I can start making calls on it first thing tomorrow Damien." By now Nicole was exiting the shower as I handed her a towel so she could dry off. "So Mr. Hustle Man, if I set these parties up for you what's my cut?"

"I got your cut right here," I replied as I groped my dick in front of her.

Nicole then gave me that devilish smile and kissed me on my lips. For that moment, I knew this would be her way of continuing to be a part of my life. I figured it would be worth it as long as the money kept rolling in for a while. Nicole quickly got dressed, brushed her teeth, and fixed her hair all within a few minutes. We said our goodbyes as if our threesome love affair was back on track again. Then Nicole departed my house and made her way back to her husband.

Chapter 21

It had been a week now since my last sexual encounter with crazy Nicole. As expected she followed up with all her girlfriends and they were eager to see what designer products I had. Since I still was waiting on Mookie to obtain the products, I simply told Nicole to set up the purse and shoe party a few weeks out. She loved the idea of putting a party together and figuring out the logistics and details. I guess it was just her marketing skills she loved to put to use. The fact that the party was another way for her to keep tabs on me didn't help.

In the meantime, I put together my own market research plan together. Maybe I was over emphasizing the whole idea of selling fenced goods, but I had to take the business approach anyway. It was going to separate me from being a good or great businessman. I tried to utilize my business skills in all aspects of life.

First, I went online and researched all the major designers and familiarized myself with their products and target audiences. Secondly, I randomly walked through Phipps Plaza, where all the celebrities in Atlanta shopped, and observed who was carrying what type of purse or wearing what brand of shoes. Third, I would stroll into Bloomingdales, Neiman Marcus, and Saks taking a peek at the hottest purses and shoes they had on display for sale. I even went so far to talk with the sales associates in each store asking which products were the best sellers and why. Finally, I went to Barnes and Noble and picked up a few women fashion magazines so I could get a visual of what were the latest styles. Most people would probably think I was nuts or going too far on my research quest just to sell purses and shoes, but I wanted to make my entrepreneur experience a true business. In order to be a good salesman you had to be a better marketer.

When Saturday afternoon arrived, I received a call from Mookie stating he wanted to check out Old School Saturday. This was an event held once a month at an upscale hotel usually in downtown Atlanta. The event consisted of large crowds who gathered to mingle, drink, and dance to R&B and rap music from the 80's and 90's. On this particular Saturday, the event was at the Hyatt Hotel located downtown on Courtland Street. I figured Mookie wanted to see some sexy females as I couldn't blame him. He had been locked up for the last ten years and I knew he needed to get his dick wet if he hadn't done so by now.

By 11:00 p.m., I had picked up Mookie from his mother's house in Decatur so we could make it to the event by midnight when it really got crowded. I figured we have a few hours to party since the event shuts down by 2:00 a.m. When we arrived at the Hyatt, I had my car valet so we wouldn't have to deal with the exiting crowd later that night. Once inside the venue, we noticed the place was packed with fine honies and the dj was getting the dance floor hype playing "Gin and Juice" by Snoop Dogg. The song was an anthem back in the day when I was a senior at Crenshaw High. It still got people rushing to the dance floor ready to shake their ass. We continued to check out the scene while heading to the bar for a cocktail.

"So Mookie, what do you want to drink?" I asked.

"Just give me a cranberry juice on the rocks," he shouted over the loud music.

"Okay," I replied not trying to look dismayed. I sure didn't want to put any pressure on Mookie drinking so I played it safe and ordered a ginger ale for myself.

When our beverages arrived, a sexy female pulled me onto the dance floor and wanted to groove to Snoop's track before it ended. As we made our way onto the dance floor, Mookie gave me a smile while holding up his cranberry juice as to give a cheer. While dancing, I noticed Mookie mingling with a few sexy females near the bar and was glad he was enjoying himself. The dj was playing all the great old school rap hits from my high school days that brought back great memories. Thus, me and my sexy female companion continue to dance through a few more songs and got more acquainted with each other. We finally exited the dance floor and I told my dance partner I would catch up with her later. She quickly slipped me her business card which I placed in my front pocket of my slacks and we said our goodbyes to each other. I wanted to make sure Mookie was alright and wasn't overwhelmed with the event.

"I'm ready to go, Casanova," exclaimed a voice from behind my back.

As I turned around, I noticed it was Mookie. Apparently, he had been watching me depart with my dance companion a few moments earlier. "We only been here maybe an hour," I replied. "Besides it's just getting right in here."

"Come on Damien, I'll tell you more outside."

As we departed the hotel's ballroom, I figured Mookie probably just wasn't feeling the party scene anymore since we were both much older now and no longer in college. When we got outside, I handed the valet my ticket as we waited for my car to pull up.

"Damien, my main purpose here tonight was just to see what trends and styles were hot for the ladies," said Mookie. "I guess you could say it was for business purposes since I have some merchandise coming in."

"Really?" I replied back. Then it dawned on me that Mookie was taking his new venture of entrepreneurship seriously and doing his homework just like me. I couldn't blame him one bit but was proud of his efforts.

"Yeah man, I should have the goods in a few days and just wanted to be prepared on what to select," he said. "Besides first comes the cash then comes the ass, you dig."

"Yeah I dig, Mookie," I said as we both starting laughing.

Driving home Mookie and I compared our research notes and strategy on how to market and sell our products. We even laughed together when I told him how I purchased the women fashion magazines. I was glad Mookie had matured and was on a business level all about money. You can't achieve anything in life without that powerful dollar.

Before we arrived at Mookie's mom house, we stopped at an I-Hop and had breakfast while continuing to talk business and the good old college days in Miami. We both ordered a full round of breakfast food which included pancakes, sausage, bacon, omelets, grits, and toast. It was obvious to our server we were men who could put away food.

By now, I was even more hyped up about generating sales from the merchandise and couldn't wait until the products came in. My new found hustle was bound to be a success.

Chapter 22

The following Saturday had arrived and just as Mookie promised the merchandise was delivered. I eagerly met with Mookie and selected all the latest designer pursers and shoes any woman would go crazy for. His inventory was better than I could have imagined. I selected all the hottest products like Gucci, Coach, Chanel, Prada, Louis Vuitton, DKNY, and Jimmy Choo just to name a few. The merchandise I selected were originals headed to major retailers but now it was obvious they weren't going to make it there. Even the retailer's tags were on the products which made the lure more lucrative. Mookie's supply man just wanted to get rid of the fenced goods ASAP, so I was able to negotiate a great deal all for wholesale prices. Once I sold the merchandise for two or three times what I paid for it my profit margin would shoot through the roof.

My initial investment was two thousand dollars which I managed to squeeze out of Nicole. Since our love affair was back on track again, so was my mandatory minimum of perks which in this case was cash. She even managed to fully set up and help host the purse and shoe party at her girlfriend's house set for next week.

My plan for today was to target a few hair salons around Atlanta and try to unload as much merchandise as I could. The first salon on my itinerary was an upscale, yet hip, salon called Styles located on

Piedmont Road. Styles' was a modern sleek and slick salon usually patroned by professional business women. Since Atlanta was now the weave capital of the world, the salons were always packed especially on Saturdays. Ironically, Nicole turned me on to this salon as it was where she had her weave tighten up every other week like clockwork.

When I pulled up to the salon, I parked my car in a less conspicuous spot. I didn't want to just carry all the merchandise into the salon and be unprofessional about my business. So I figured I would at least ask the owner if I could solicit the customers first. Before I walked in, I placed an unisex Gucci messenger bag around my torso so the customers would see a sample of my product line. I was again using my marketing skills in order to gain their attention for sales. I also knew no one in Atlanta had ever seen the new bag before as it was only available via the Gucci Store in selected cities. As I walked through the front door, a young lady greeted me promptly.

"Hello handsome," she said. "Are you here for a scheduled trim?"

"Actually no," I replied as I noticed how attractive she was. As I look around momentarily, I realized all the women working in the salon were quite attractive. It was like an epidemic in there. "I'm here to see the owner about some business products if possible."

"Okay sure, what's your name?"

"I'm Damien Hardy"

"Well Damien, it's nice to meet you and by the way I'm Tameka."

"Tameka, the pleasure is all mine," I said with a charming smile.

"Ms. Graham, who is the owner, is in the rear of the salon," Tameka said smiling back at me. "I'll introduce you to her just follow me."

"Sounds good Tameka and thanks for all your help," I replied as I followed her.

As we walked through the salon, I couldn't help but notice all the beautiful and fashionable women getting their hair taken care of. They all took notice of my messenger bag as if was different and eye catching since it was a Gucci. Either that or the fact I was the only man in the whole salon. When we finally made it to the rear part of the salon, I could see Ms. Graham who had her back towards us. Even from her backside I knew she was fine as hell. She was placing a customer under a professional dryer. Her attire included a sexy sun dress which showed all the right curves and was complimented by a pair of Gucci heels. I could spot a pair of high end shoes from any distance as I learned this from my days working at Macy's. Her hair was long and blonde which came right to her shoulders. I figured at least we both liked Gucci and maybe I could use that as an icebreaker.

"Ms. Graham, there is a gentleman by the name of Mr. Hardy here to see you about some business products," said Tameka. Ms. Graham turned around to face us quickly.

"Damien!" she shouted.

"Diamond!" I yelled in a whisper of excitement and surprise.

"Oh, I see you two must know each other," said Tameka as she looked with a bit of confusion on her face. "Well, I'll let you two get reacquainted." Then Tameka turned and walked away but not before she gave me a wink.

"Damien baby, how have you been doing?" asked Diamond as we hugged passionately right there in the salon for all to see. By now nearly everyone was turning their heads wondering who was this guy hugging the owner.

"I've been good," I remarked. "I see your not doing to bad for yourself. You always said you wanted to start your own business."

"Thank you baby," she said. "Let's go into my office where we can have more privacy and catch up on where we left off." Suddenly Diamond grabbed my hand and whisked me off in excitement. We ended up in her office nearby which was a decent size. She took a seat behind her large mahogany desk and offered me a seat in plush leather chair.

"So Damien, how long has it been? I think maybe ten years. What have you been doing with your life?"

"I was working for Coca-Cola for the last ten years until the recession finally caught up with the company and my position was terminated. But that's not interesting, I want to know what's been going on with you, Diamond?"

"Well for one no one calls me Diamond anymore," she said in a low whisper. "Everyone in here calls me Ms. Graham or Renee as they don't know I use to dance when I was attending Spelman College."

"Okay, I can respect that," I said.

"But you can still can me Diamond only behind closed doors," she said as we both started smiling. "Anyway right after graduating from college, I moved back to Chicago and began working for a major financial institution as an investment banker for the next five years. Then I mustard enough courage to step out on faith and start my own salon on the South Side of Chicago."

"So how long have you been back in Atlanta?" I asked eagerly.

"I just relocated my salon business here, early this year, in February," she said. "I needed a change of scenery and felt Atlanta offered a great hair market. Well enough about me, Tameka said you wanted to discuss some business products. Are you in the hair salon market now?"

"No, not exactly Diamond. With the scarcity of jobs right now I decided to try my hand at selling high end designer merchandise like purses and shoes."

"Did you say designer purses and shoes, Damien?"

"Yeah that's right," I said smiling a bit.

"Oh baby, please bring your products into the salon," she said. "My customers are always looking for the latest fashion deals. Besides I had to kick a guy out of here two weeks ago for showing us some inferior products."

Before I went to retrieve the merchandise from my car, I exchanged phone numbers with Diamond. We both promised to meet up for dinner in a few days and finish getting reacquainted again. I never bothered to ask if she was involved with anyone as I figure she would have said something if she was. Diamond was still the same down to earth person I knew ten years ago with that same passion for making money. She didn't let the success of her business turn her into an arrogant woman and I liked that.

When I returned back from my car with the merchandise, it was like Christmas in July. It started with me showing one woman a Gucci handbag sold exclusively at Bloomingdales. Within seconds other women were asking to see my products and what I had to offer. I felt like a kid in a candy store as there was a buying frenzy. One woman even made her stylist stop washing her hair so she wouldn't miss out on someone else buying the Prada shoes she wanted. At one point, I felt like I was working at Macy's again when the woman started trying on all the designer shoes I brought in. Luckily, I have enough sizes in seven and eight as they were the most common for women. Back when I was working at Macy's I could look at a woman's foot and instantly tell what size she worn. Now that trait was coming back in handy. By the time I left Diamond's salon, I had sold twelve purses and nine pair of shoes. It was an easy "lick" as we use to say back in L.A. I even gave Diamond a complimentary Gucci purse that matched the heels she was wearing.

Later that afternoon, I repeated the same process at various salons throughout Atlanta. Most of the salons were friendly and supported me and my hustle. My products were so superior the women didn't even think about passing up a good deal. If I paid fifty dollars for a purse at wholesale I usually sold it for one hundred or one hundred and fifty dollars. This same purse easily sold for three hundred dollars at any given mall because my merchandise was original and not a knockoff. I was able to make money hand over fist and exceed my profit margin for every product. No other booster or street vendor could complete with my inventory or prices and women took notice of this quick. I even went back to my old neighborhood on Candler Road and hit a few salons in the area. Hell, I didn't discriminate what town of side I conducted business on. From Bankhead to Buckhead it really didn't matter because in the end money was green.

By dusk, I was beat and was headed back to Buckhead as I travel on Greenbrier Parkway leaving a salon in the area. I only had maybe two purses and one pair of shoes left in my truck from the start of the day. Before jumping back on I-285, I pulled into to parking lot of a Jamaican Restaurant as I had a taste for some jerk chicken served over brown rice. I could smell the savoring flavor from my car. I figured I would place a to go order and eat my meal from the confines of my condo as I was tired. Before I entered the establishment I pulled all the money from my front pockets of my Ralph Lauran jeans and began to count. Amazingly, I had made thirty-three hundred dollars for the day. I even counted the money twice as I could believe how easily I made it. My new found hustle was definitely a good way to supplement my income.

As I walked up to the restaurant, I noticed a space of land that was cleared a few yards away. Construction had begun and the building was almost complete. There was a sign which read: Coming Soon: General Family Medical Practice. I noticed how odd as there were no other medical facilities in this general location. I thought it was a good idea as medical care could benefit the community and keep people from traveling so far to obtain it. I then turned my attention back to the restaurant, licked my lips, and proceeded to enter the front door.

Chapter 23

A few weeks had passed since my very first day selling purses and shoes at various salons in Atlanta. By now, I had a patented routine how, when, and where to sell my products. For example, I would travel to a certain salon on a Friday or Saturday then go back to that same salon two weeks later. This would allow the women to enjoy their products for a few weeks. When they got their paychecks again, they were ready to buy just as before. If I didn't frequent one salon I was busy visiting another, then another, and so on. But I always came back to the salon I missed previously. It was a good system I had going because the women never got tired of seeing me too often.

Mookie had an even better system set up for distribution. By now, he had managed to recruit a few other budding entrepreneurs who purchased wholesale from him. These individuals had their own shops and clothing boutiques out of state and linked up with Mookie every few weeks for new merchandise. He was careful not to saturate the Atlanta market too much with his product as he wanted me to corner the market first. Besides everyone else in Atlanta had the knockoffs and Mookie's connection had the real deal merchandise. Apparently, his connection had an inside man at the Port of Miami. The crew would knock off various containers or trucks before they departed for the major retailers. By now, I was following up with Mookie every week.

On this particular Saturday night, I had Nicole working a purse and shoe party she set up at her girlfriend's house. The word was out that these high end designer products were all the rave and a must see. I had even let Nicole flaunt a few purses to work to showcase what would be at the purse and shoe party. This strategy worked exactly as planned. Once one woman saw her purses she would inquire and that started a chain reaction of women wanting to know how she could get her hands on one or two. Nicole was an expert in marketing and planned to have about fifty women at the event. She would have cocktails and serve appetizers for everyone as well. I didn't want to stand around and listen to a bunch of tipsy catty women fight over which shoes or purse to buy. So instead, I met Nicole earlier in the day and allowed her to select from my inventory all the merchandise she could take to the party. She knew what type of styles her corporate girlfriends wanted. By the time she left, her Cadillac Escalade was fully packed with boxes of merchandise. Nicole got a high on doing anything that benefited me. Plus, as always, she could still maintain her connection with me. For putting the party together I promised her two complimentary purses and shoes. She was ecstatic at my gesture but told me she wanted some hard dick on top of that.

Since Nicole would be busy for the rest of the night with the party I made plans to get reacquainted with Diamond. She had been extremely busy working long hours at her solon, but I guess it was the price to pay for owning your own business. We constantly talked on each other on our cell phones since I first saw her again at the salon. We even tripped out about all the previous hot passionate sex we had, especially the first time we hooked up. By now, I was craving for her again wondering was the pussy still as good as before.

We made plans to meet at Sambuca's in the Buckhead district of Atlanta. Sambuca specialized in upscale, fine dining with a live jazz band. This would be the perfect place for us to sip on cocktails, eat a wonderful meal, and enjoy the ambiance with the live music. I had made dinner reservations for ten o'clock and was now looking through my closet trying to decide what to wear. I finally opted for my conservative attire which included navy blue Ralph Lauren slacks with a patterned dress shirt. My accessories would include white gold cufflinks and an ascot which would set me apart from all the hating brothers. I would don a dark taupe blazer and black Gucci penny loafers which never seemed to go out of style.

By nine forty-five, I was fully dressed and headed on my way to the restaurant. Since I already lived in Buckhead, I was only a few minutes away. My black bimmer was fully detailed with my chrome twenty-two inch rims blinging even at night.

I even managed to pick up a single pink rose for Diamond earlier in the day. Pink was her favorite color as I remembered it was throughout her condo ten years earlier. As I cruised on Peachtree Road nearing Piedmont, my BlackBerry began to vibe. Before I looked at who was calling me I prayed it wasn't Nicole. I didn't want to be disturbed with her as I knew she was probably feeling good off a few cocktails by now. As I looked on my cell phone the incoming call had a Los Angeles area code.

"Hello," I said.

"Hey boo boo! It's Raphael your cousin from L.A."

I hadn't heard from Raphael in years as he always had a trait of vanishing then calling people up on a whim. I always had the same cell phone number since I lived in Atlanta. Apparently, he never forgot it.

"What's going on with you, Raphael?" I asked. "How are things in L.A.?"

"Everything is grand Damien, but I'm in a transition of trying to relocate to Atlanta."

"Well what brought on that idea?"

"I just need a change of scenery and besides I have an interview with a professional salon there next week."

"That's cool Raphael, I hope everything works out for you. I think you'll like Atlanta although it's a little watered down compared to L.A and the cost of living is much more inexpensive."

"Well since you mentioned living, I wanted to ask you if I could stay at your place for a few days while I'm in Atlanta for my interview."

"You know that's no problem, Raphael. I'll even be able to pick you from the airport too."

"Thanks so much Damien, you've always been there for me when nobody else was. I'll text you my flight info closer to my arrival date."

"C'mon man, you know were cousins and suppose to be there for each other."

"So what does Mr. Ladies' Man have plan for tonight?"

"Actually, I'm on my way to meet someone for dinner at Sambuca's. You know I'm no ladies' man, Raphael."

"Yeah right Damien, you have always been so modest. I know your handling those sex-deprived women down there in Hotlanta, especially with the shortage of men in that city. You ought to go out with me to Club Bulldogs when I come to town."

"I never heard of that spot. What type of club is it anyway?"

"It's an all gay men club in midtown silly, you know how I do boo. Besides all those down low brothers would get jealous once they saw me walking in the club with you."

"You know I don't get down like that," I said laughing hysterically. "But I appreciate the offer."

"Chi please, you know I'm just messing with you Damien. I'll talk to you soon. Chow."

"Okay Raphael and be safe. Peace."

By now, I was pulling up to the entrance of Sambuca. Before I exited my vehicle, I remembered to grab the single pink rose for Diamond which was lying on the passenger's side seat. It was ten o'clock on the dot and I was on time as usual. I took the parking ticket from the valet and made my way to the front entrance where a female hostess smiled and greeted me.

"Oh, how sweet of you! Thank you for my rose," exclaimed the attractive young hostess.

"Well, actually the rose is for my date," I said blushing and smiling simultaneously.

"I know, I was just kidding with you," she replied. "How many will be dining with you tonight, sir?"

"Just one other person. I made reservations for two under Hardy at ten o'clock."

"Yes sir, I have you here on the list. Has your date arrived?"

"No, I don't think so yet," I said while I overlooked the restaurant for Diamond.

"Feel free to enjoy a drink at our bar until your date arrives, sir. I'll be glad to seat you at your table then."

"That sounds like a good idea. I think I will enjoy a cocktail at the bar, thank you."

As I made my way to the bar with the rose handled very carefully, all the guys with their female dates were giving me the jealous look. They were wondering why they didn't think to bring a rose for their dates too. The rose symbolized a romantic evening for a night to come and I gathered much attention with it. When I sat down at the bar the bartender quickly took my order.

"And what will you be drinking tonight, sir?"

"Hennessey with ginger ale."

"Yes sir, coming right up."

Waiting for my drink, I received a text from Diamond which read: *Sorry baby, I'm running a little late. See you in ten minutes.* Although I'm not a text fan, I gladly texted Diamond back with the response: *It's ok. At the bar having a drink.*

By the time Diamond arrived, I had finished my drink and had a slight buzz but felt relaxed. I knew she had arrived because all the brothers at the bar were gawking at her with their eyes nearly bursting out their heads. I even heard one guy ask his friend, "Man who is that fine ass stallion coming through the door?" I remained seated as I allowed Diamond to make her entrance and continue to turn heads at the same time. Right on cue she noticed me patiently sitting at the bar and made her way over.

"Hello baby," said Diamond. "Sorry to keep you waiting."

"Aw no problem," I replied as I stood up to greet and hug her. "I really just got here not too long ago myself."

She was dressed stunning as ever but to no surprise. Her lightly colored pastel dress was provocative but classy. It hugged her ass as if it was tailor made. Of course, she wore a pair of four-inch Gucci heels which were her trademark brand. Her natural beauty complimented her blond colored hair which flowed all the way down near her protruding breasts.

"Nice diamond-laced necklace," I said trying to direct my eyes away from her breasts.

"Thank you," she responded. "And don't you look debonair sporting your ascot and blazer."

"Well you know it was just a little something different I pulled out of the closet for you," I said. We both laughed and smiled at each other as we knew we were dressed to impress. Right then I handed her the rose I bought which was still lying on the bar. "This is for you, Diamond."

"Thanks sweetheart, you're a true gentleman," replied Diamond with empathy. "How did you remember pink was my favorite color after all these years?"

"Well sometimes a man never forgets certain things," I said.

Right then I took Diamond by her hand and led her back to the hostess so we could be seated. It was perfect timing as the jazz band was beginning to perform their first set for the night. Graciously, our hostess gave us a table right in the front of the band but far away enough where we could have some privacy. On cue, our server then came over and introduced herself. She recommended the sea bass skewers as an appetizer as we overlooked our menus. We agreed to the appetizers and then I ordered a Moscado for Diamond and a Heineken for myself. While we waited for our drinks and appetizers I struck up a conversation with her.

"So Diamond, how are things going with the salon?"

"Very busy Damien, but I like the fast pace environment as it makes the day fly by and keeps everyone occupied."

"Do you like having a salon here in Atlanta versus Chicago?"

"Well I only been here less than a year, but I think I like the atmosphere in Atlanta more. I just wish I had one or two more male stylists to add a little diversity to my salon."

"As a matter of fact my cousin, who is a stylist in L.A., is flying into Atlanta next week for a job interview," I said. "I could have him meet with you if you're up to it."

"That would be great," she exclaimed. "I would love to meet him and discuss his credentials if he's interested."

"My cousin's name is Raphael," I slightly shouted as the band began to play a little louder.

"Thanks Damien, I really appreciate that. I'll look forward to hearing from him soon."

Our server returned back to our table with our drinks and appetizers. In the interim, Diamond had already decided what she wanted to eat and so did I. Being a true gentleman, I placed Diamond's selection for her which consisted of blackened tilapia served with jasmine rice and spicy cream sauce. For myself, I chose the stuffed chicken, which was a pan seared chicken breast stuffed with crab and shrimp topped with lemon cream sauce over smashed potatoes.

While we waited for our entrées, Diamond and I sipped on our cocktails, enjoyed the appetizers, and laughed about the days back in '98. The establishment was jammed packed while we listened to classic melodies. Even a few couples got up and danced on a make shift dance floor in front of the band. After their dance was complete everyone applauded their efforts. I on the other hand was too busy noticing how beautiful Diamond was. She glowed with radiant energy and seemed to have not aged a bit or lost her fantastic figure.

Just as I decided to get more personal with Diamond and ask her if she had a significant other in her life, our food had arrived. Once we had our designated plates, I held Diamond's hand and blessed the food. As expected, I devoured my meal as if I had never eaten a day in my life. Diamond remanded to her girly girl mode which took her a little longer to finish. After another round of cocktails we both were relaxed and ready for whatever awaited us.

"So Ms. Diamond, as attractive and successful as you are, I know you have a special person in your life."

"Yes, you could say I definitely have a special person in my life. C'mon, let's dance."

Before I could ask any further questions, Diamond had grabbed my hand and whisked me onto the dance floor. The band was now playing "Forever My Lady" by Jodeci. Diamond and I were slowly dancing while hugged up to each other. I smoothly kissed her right earlobe and then moved down her neck not caring if the other patrons were watching.

"All right now, don't start something you can't finish," she said.

"You know that never pertained to me," I said. "Besides I think it's time for us to get out of here and relax back at my place. I'm only a few minutes away."

"Okay baby, that sounds great," she said while looking into my eyes with her seductive stare.

We both walked back over to our table just as other couples were joining in on the dance floor. As we sat down, I motioned for our server to bring our check. After I paid for dinner, we both obtained our cars from valet as I told Diamond to simply follow me back to my condo near Lenox Road. Diamond still had her classy taste in cars as she was sporting a black BMW X5 with the thirty-five percent tint, of course. Before we pulled off, she complimented me on my BMW 745i knowing I came along way from the old Nissan Maximum I once had.

By now, it was almost midnight as Diamond trailed me while traveling on Piedmont Road. Suddenly, I received a text from Nicole stating: *party was a success, want to cum c u*. I was in no mood to deal with Nicole who was probably tipsy by now and horny as hell. I wasn't even going to think about passing up Diamond for the night. I simply deleted Nicole's text and kept driving.

When we arrived at my condo, I directed Diamond to park in the designated space for visitors. She quickly complied and then jumped in my car as I sped through the parking garage to my parking spot. After which we rode the elevator to the twelfth floor and it seemed like déjà vu again. As we entered my condo, instantly we began to kiss each other passionately. I grabbed Diamond's breasts and easily moved down the top of her dress sucking on her nipples.

"Damien baby that feels so good!" she shouted. "But I really need to tell you something about the special person in my life."

"I'm okay with it if you are," I said while lifting up her dress and rubbing her thick ass. "He's not here now and I promise not to tell."

"Silly, I know he's not here," Diamond responded. "Actually, he's back in Chicago with my mother."

"Huh!" I said as the mood quickly shifted between us. "What do you mean he's with your mother?"

"Damien that special person in my life is named Christian and he's my son. He'll be nine years old this year."

The mood was more serious as I moved myself off of her. We both stood there in the dark foyer of my condo simply looking at each other. What seemed to be an eternity of thoughts only lasted a few seconds.

"Diamond, I'm cool with that, just as long as I don't have to deal with any baby daddy drama."

"No Damien, you still don't get it," she said placing up her hands. "Christian is your son too!"

Chapter 24

"Got damnit, move it!" I screamed at the traffic in front of me. I was on the downtown connector headed towards Hartsfield-Jackson Airport to pick up Raphael. His plane was scheduled to arrive at 1:05 p.m. as I looked at my watch. I had less than twenty minutes to make it to the airport on time. I was beyond frustrated as I left my condo in ample time but had been stuck in traffic for almost an hour. To make matters worse, there was a slow moving Marta bus in front of my car obscuring my view. "What the hell is a damn Marta bus doing on the interstate?" I said out loud to myself. I thought they were supposed to travel on surface streets only.

I had been on edge and temperamental for the last few days ever since Diamond dropped the bombshell on me I was the father of her son. That night at my condo she told me she didn't know she was two months pregnant until the end of April back in '99. By then, she had graduated from Spelman College and moved back to Chicago. She did admit to sleeping with more men than just me, but only our sex was unprotected. When the baby was born she said all my characteristics were evident and she knew he was my son. Diamond further told me she named the child Christian as she became more spiritual and closer to a higher power. I asked her why she didn't tell me about the child earlier. Her response was that she felt guilty on how his birth had transpired and figured she could raise him alone. Now she realized the child needed a father in his life. All this was quite a pill to swallow with the challenges I was already facing but I knew I had to man up if indeed Christian was my son. I couldn't fault Diamond for being promiscuous in the past as I wasn't any better. But I wasn't ruling out a DNA test just to legitimize the child was mine.

By now, traffic was finally beginning to move again as I had traveled all the way past Turner Field Stadium. There was an overturned car in the far left lane with another damage car next to it. Paramedics were on the scene while the Atlanta Police Department was directing traffic. Cars were moving at a snail's pace as the rubberneckers were out in full effect. Even I sneaked a peak at the wreckage. As I whizzed by, I pressed on the car's accelerator moving past the commotion knowing Raphael's plane would be landing anytime now. Quickly, I sent him a text stating I was running a little late due to traffic but would meet him in baggage claim as we discussed previously.

At precisely 1:30 p.m., I was turning into the Atlanta Airport exit. I figured once I parked my car and walked to baggage claim Raphael would be arriving there as well. He still had to make the trek from the gate which was quite some distance. I quickly found a parking spot and briskly walked into the terminal headed to baggage claim. I was anxious to see my cousin as I last saw him in '93 when we graduated from Crenshaw High. Back then Raphael, who was known as Ralph, was a tall, shy, chubby kid with glasses who I protected. We were complete opposites as I was athletic, popular, and smart. Raphael was out of shape, a square, and didn't accept academics seriously.

Just as soon as the thoughts of past high school days crossed my mind, I saw Raphael standing in baggage claim as I walked closer. Surprisingly, he looked nothing like the kid I remembered in high school. His fat was now replaced with muscles as his erect six-four frame supported his stature. He had to at least weigh two-hundred and thirty pounds from what I could tell but he was solid and cut up like Ving Rhames. Yeah, that's right I said Ving Rhames, even I had to do a double take. His flamboyant side was a dead giveaway about his sexuality as he sported a pink scarf around his neck, white D&G sunglasses, skinny jeans, trendy heels, and what seemed to be a man purse.

"What's up, cousin!" I yelled out as I crept up on him before he noticed me.

"Damien, how good to see you boo!" he said turning to me and giving me a warm big hug. Then he pretended to kiss my left cheek followed by my right one as if we were in France. "You look great Damien, I see you're still in shape after all these years.

"Well, you know I always been a health and fitness fanatic," I replied. "Hey man, look at you. I see you definitely bulked up since our high school days. It's a complete metamorphisms but you look great!"

"Oh honey it was a little something my personal trainer helped me with among other things when I was back in San Fran," he replied with a devilish grin. "Back then my self esteem was low but being able to work out changed all that."

"I see," I said smiling. "So have your bags arrived yet?"

"Not yet but they should be here shortly," Raphael said as we continued to watch the baggage carousel.

Finally, his bags came up from the slow moving carousel. I grabbed his large suitcase while Raphael retrieved his smaller travel bag. You would have thought he was staying with me for a month by the way his bag weighed as I positioned myself to carry it.

"Damn cuz, I thought you said you were only staying for a few days. This bag must weigh at least sixty pounds."

"Oh Damien, please stop complaining. Besides, I didn't know what to wear so I brought a few extra items. You know what they say about traveling?

"No Raphael, what do they say?"

"A diva must be a diva and be prepared at all times!"

We were making our way out the airport towards my car and I noticed a few heads turning and stares. Apparently, some people thought we were a couple and even snickered and laughed under their breath, of course. I maintained focused on getting out of the airport and tried not to let other's ignorance bothered me. When I looked over at Raphael it was as if he didn't notice anything or didn't even care.

"So how was your fight?" I asked trying to diffuse the situation as we continued to walk.

"If it wasn't for a few shots of Grey Goose I don't know how I would have made it through the four hour flight," he said laughing. "Once we touched down in the ATL I think I was the first person running off the plan. I can't stand long flights it makes me so nervous."

After we walked through a cross walk and maneuvered through the parking lot we finally made it to my car. I was thankful Raphael's luggage had wheels or else I would have suffered from a hernia by now. As we got near the car, I opened the trunk with the remove on my key ring.

"Well here we are," I said.

"I see you came a long way from your Datsun days, he said. "Is this you?"

"Yeah, this is all me. Something I worked hard for after all those years working for Coca-Cola."

"I didn't think selling shoes at Macy's would yield you a tight bimmer," he said trying to make fun at me.

"Hell no, you got that right," I replied. "I left Macy's ten years ago and worked at Coke ever since in their marketing department. I was let go recently due to budget constraints. Well at least that is what they told me."

"Damien, I'm so sorry to hear that."

"Don't be," I said as I finished placing Raphael's bags in my car's truck. "I got a new hustle on life that gives me more money, freedom, and flexibility."

"And what might that be?" he asked.

"Get in Raphael, I'll explain it all to you later."

We made it through the downtown connector just in time to beat the normal traffic delays and melee that has plagued Atlanta for years. Raphael felt like cheating on his fitness and health by asking me to stop by In-N-Out Burger. I know he was teasing me because he knew good and got damn well In-N-Out Burger was exclusively located in Los Angeles. Turning the table on him, I drove up to Krystal's drive thru where he simply turned up his nose. We both decided to eat healthy and grabbed a bite to eat at Boston Market on North Druid Hills Road which was minutes from my condo.

By the time I drove back to my place, the sun was beginning to set and we figured to call it a day as Raphael had an interview the next afternoon. I even managed to tell him about Diamond's salon and how she was looking for some male stylists to bring more atmosphere to her establishment. After I gave him Diamond's salon number, he promised to follow up with her no later than tomorrow. He was only in town until Sunday and wanted to take advantage of every employment opportunity that was available.

As we were taking the elevator to my condo, I received a text from Nicole stating she was in the vicinity and was planning to stop by. With the surprise Diamond flaunted on me Saturday night, I had forgotten to follow back up with Nicole regarding the results of the party. More importantly, I needed to collect my paper she earned for me. I also figured she wanted her normal dose of medicine since she had now contributed to my hustle.

I had made sure my condo was cleaned and new sheets were on the bed in the second bedroom for Raphael. I wanted him to feel as comfortable as possible while he was visiting me in Atlanta. As we entered my unit, Raphael was pleased, shocked, and surprised.

"Okay Mr. Bachelor, I see you've done quite well with your living arrangements since you left L.A.," he said. "I really like how you decorated the place. It has a masculine theme but a hint of a women as if one decorated for you."

"No way," I replied. "Believe it or not I did it all myself. I picked out the furniture, color schemes, and accessories."

"Boi stop!" Raphael said in his animated tone while shaking his head. "You killing me thinking you designed this up in here."

"It's all true Raphael. I have no reason to lie to you of all people."

For the next few moments, I gave him a brief tour of my place and showed him where his bedroom was. By the time we made it to the balcony to watch the view of traffic in Buckhead, Raphael had made himself an apple martini. As always, I kept a full bar stocked with various liquors, chasers, and beer just for guest since I was no heavy drinker. He sipped on his cocktail while I drank a ginger ale. As we watch the view below, my doorbell rang and I knew it could only be Nicole. I excused myself from the balcony and answered the door.

"Hello stranger, where have you been hiding for the last few days?" Nicole asked still standing in the doorway. She was still dressed in her normal sleek business attire from Coca-Cola and was looking stunning as usual.

"What's up, Nicole?" I replied back. "You know I've been busy with the usual day to day activities."

"Uh huh, yeah right," she answered back with an attitude.

"C'mon in and join me on the balcony, I want to introduce you to my cousin." She stepped inside and we made our way to were Raphael was.

"Hey Girl, I love your Jimmy Choo purse and heels that match," was the first thing Raphael said to Nicole as we walked onto the balcony.

"Oh thank you," she responded with a big smile.

During the quick pause in communication I made the proper introduction with each of them. It was quite unnecessary as Raphael was no longer shy and blended in well with everyone he met now.

"It's so nice to meet you sweetie," he said. Then without any hesitation Raphael hugged Nicole and pretended to kiss her left cheek saying "muuuah" in the process. He repeated the same process to her right cheek as well not forgetting to say "muuuah" also. "You must tell me where you got your purse and heels cause I never seen that style before."

"You don't know?" asked Nicole. "I got them from your cousin himself, Mr. Hustler," she said smiling.

"Oh Damien, I didn't know you were in the import and export business."

"Yeah Raphael, I replied. "I'm supplementing my limited income selling designer purses and shoes."

"Well boo I ain't mad at ya," Raphael exclaimed. "I just know I need to get me a Jimmy Choo purse before I leave back for L.A."

Nicole and I laughed at Raphael and his flamboyant attitude as he kept it real as it could be. Despite his sexuality, he wasn't afraid to show it. By now, Nicole was so comfortable she even had Raphael make her an apple martini.

"So Nicole, you gonna hang out with me at Club Bulldogs before I go back to L.A.?" Raphael asked.

"Sure Raphael, that's no problem. I haven't been there in a few years, but I'm open to revisit it again."

"So Nicole, you been to Club Bulldogs before?" I asked.

"Yes Damien. One of my girlfriends had an itch to see what the club was all about one night, so we got dressed and had a ball. All the guys were cool and made us feel so comfortable."

"Wonderful girl!" shouted Raphael while clapping his hands. "You can be my chaperone when we go. I need someone to keep me in line so I won't act out too bad while in Atlanta."

Raphael was into his full spectacle by now and Nicole loved every minute of it. I didn't know if she was into his animated attitude or if she never met anyone with quite the flare as he had. But I guess it really didn't matter because as the evening went on, both of them seem to be more comfortable with one another.

Raphael, was probably something different for Nicole as she wouldn't have to worry about him stealing her man. Every woman in Atlanta knew you couldn't bring just any of your girlfriends around someone you were involved with. With the male shortage and all, your girlfriend could quickly try to move in on the action. If a woman found a gem and wanted to keep him all for herself, she played it safe by not bringing any of her girlfriends around him.

I kind of liked it though as I figured maybe Nicole could take some of all that unwanted attention she was given me, and exert it onto Raphael. As far as I was concern, they could be the best hang out buddies while he was in Atlanta.

We all eventually moved inside to the living room to watch television as the hazel sky turned dark. The apple martini Nicole had must have taken an effect on her as she clung on me while we sat on the sofa. Discreetly, while Raphael was making himself a final drink, she whispered she wanted to give me a blow job before leaving my place. I felt compelled by her wish since she did such a good job with the party. By the time Raphael made his way back to the living room with his drink, Nicole and I excused ourselves to my bedroom for a moment. While in my bedroom she gave me a stack of cash and I let her taste me for a while. Afterwards, Nicole said a farewell to Raphael and made her way back home. Raphael and I then spent the rest of the night talking about the good old days in L.A.

Chapter 25

It was another busy and hectic Saturday as I had just wrapped up my usual rounds at various salons. I was in the Greenbriar area again. I got an early jump on my daily trek as I wanted to finish well before the evening. My motto was to work smarter not harder. If I could work four hours and make the same amount of money as working eight I was satisfied.

Besides, I had to meet with Diamond around six o'clock at her salon later today. We had to talk about Christian as I needed a few days for reality to sink in. After Diamond told me I was the father of her child, I went into a mode consisting of anger, denial, and frustration. The few days we had away from each other allowed me to gather my thoughts and think straight. The thought of me being a father was exciting and scary at the same time. Fatherhood was all new to me but I was ready for the responsibility if Christian was my blood. Maybe, I could even live out my baseball fantasy through him if he loved the sport. If he was interested, I could teach him the game of baseball and help him matriculate into the athlete I was less the injuries. But I wanted to take it slow, as I didn't know how receptive he would be. I didn't even know if he ever asked about his father or what Diamond ever said about me. One thing was for certain, I had to make up a lot of ground and fast.

Raphael's interview the day before yesterday was a success. The professional salon he had a scheduled interview with loved him. His client portfolio and presentation skills were impressive. Plus he brought a flare from the west coast the salon was in need for. So impressed was the salon, that he was offered a position.

But Diamond was even more impressed by what Raphael had to offer when he followed up with her the same day. In fact, she offered him a hefty salary, with benefits, which he couldn't resist. Now Raphael could relocate to Atlanta while working in his dream field. After he told me about Diamond's offer I extended my place for him to live while he found something on his own. Before his departure back to Los Angeles tomorrow, he and Nicole had decided to celebrate at Club Bulldogs tonight. They wanted me to join them but I declined.

Before heading back to Buckhead district of Atlanta, I decided to frequent the Jamaican restaurant I had fell in love with while working on this side of town. As usual, I had a taste for their mouth watering jerk chicken over brown rice. Today, I could actually go inside, sit down, and enjoy my meal as I had a few hours to spare before I met Diamond.

As I whipped my bimmer into the small parking lot, I noticed the two story medical practice next to the restaurant was now completed and open for business. Walking up to the restaurant, I turned to glace at the balloons and banner that aligned the front of the building. As I smiled with one hand reaching for the restaurant door, I read the banner which stated: Now Open Family Medical Clinic, Dr. Crystal Gayle. Immediately, my eyes lit up like a Christmas tree. I had to do a double take at the banner to make sure I was reading it correctly. By now, I had taken my hand off the restaurant door and was facing the medical clinic in a daze.

"Excuse us," said a couple as they attempted to make their way into the restaurant. Apparently, I was blocking their way into the entrance.

"Oh, sorry," I replied back as I walked towards the medical clinic without looking at them.

By the time I made my way to the building, I tried to convince myself this couldn't be the Crystal Gayle I once knew. No twist of fate or Hollywood script could predict this outcome. As I stood on the outside in front of the facility I continued to stare at the signage once again. Suddenly, an elderly man walking with a cane, accompanied by what seemed to be his daughter exited the front entrance. I was snapped out of my daze. I smiled and nodded to them in a friendly gesture and they both smiled back. After they passed me, I stood there in a cold sweat trying to muster enough courage to enter the building. I thought about turning away but knew that would come back to haunt me if I failed to find out whether or not this was the Crystal Gayle I had once loved so much. After I finally got up enough nerves, I entered the building to where a friendly receptionist greeted me from behind a counter.

"Hello sir," she said with a smile. "We are actually closing in few minutes. Did you have an appointment set for today?"

"Um actually no," I replied. "I'm a personal friend of Dr. Gayle and was just in the area wanting to say hi."

"I believe Dr. Gayle may be finishing up with a patient," she responded. "But let me call her office phone and see if she is available."

"Thank you very much," I said slowly and nervously.

"May I ask, what's your name sir?"

"Just let her know it's a close friend from Los Angeles,"

As the receptionist was making a call to Crystal's office I stood there in amazement. I looked around the pleasant office which was modest but comfortable. If this was Crystal's medical practice she had done pretty well for herself. At least her dreams had come true, I thought to myself.

"Sir, Dr. Gayle will be right out in a moment," she said interrupting my thoughts.

"Okay."

While waiting, I continued to look at the various artworks on the wall in the waiting area. It had been fifteen long years since that terrible day on the USC campus and I didn't even know what I was going to say to Crystal. I never had any intension of ever speaking to her again. Now, I was standing in what I believed to be her business waiting to see if indeed it was her. Suddenly, a slide door opened and I turned around quickly and noticed a little boy holding his mother's hand departing the office. Then I continue to glace at the artwork waiting patiently. Before long without any foreseeable warning, there was someone walking up behind me.

"Sir, I'm Dr. Gayle, can I be any assistance to you?"

Before I turned around, I knew instantly it was Crystal by her sweet voice. I took a deep breath, closed, and reopened my eyes and turned around facing her. The few seconds seemed like eternity.

"Oh my God!" she shouted at the top of her lungs. "Damien Hardy what are you doing here?"

"Hello Crystal," I replied calmly. "I was in the area and saw your banner outside with your name. So I decided to drop in."

As I stared into Crystal's eyes, I noticed she was still as beautiful as ever. She still had her petite cheerleader physique underneath her white doctor's lab coat. The stethoscope she had donned around her neck gave her the physician look she always aspired for. Her sandy brown hairstyle complemented her bronze toned complexion, as her conservative diamond earrings sparkled in the light.

"Damien, it's so good to see you again after all these years," she said while grabbing and hugging me at the same time.

I was so overwhelmed by her response I stood there momentarily with my arms by my side. Then I finally placed my arms around her as I hugged her back.

"Damien, you look great and still athletic as ever."

"You still look beautiful yourself, Crystal."

"Oh thank you Damien, but with all these long hours at work it's hard to keep up motivating myself to hit the gym."

"Looks like you've done a pretty well for yourself with your own medical practice," I said while looking around the facility. "You always said you wanted to have your own business one day."

"Well this facility is an extension of my medical practice in L.A.," Crystal replied. "The L.A. location is being run by my business partner as we decided to branch out to Atlanta."

While Crystal was talking and motioning her hands during the conversation I noticed she did not have a wedding ring on.

"Your business should perform very well in the Atlanta market Crystal or should I say Dr. Gayle."

"Oh stop that, Damien," said Crystal smiling back with laughter while hitting me on my arm in a playful mood. "You know I'll always be Crystal to you."

"I know you're pretty busy and all but I thought maybe you could join me for a quick bite to eat next door at the Jamaican restaurant," I said as the mood turned serious. "We could bury the hatchet and catch up on what's new."

"Yes, Mr. Hardy, I would love to bury the hatchet with you and grab something to eat next door," she said while seductively grinning. "Let me guess, jerk chicken for you, right?"

"You still remembered after all these years," I replied as we both laughed.

"How could I forget," she exclaimed. "You made me remember all the places that sold jerk chicken in L.A. while we were dating. Let me just tell my colleagues I'm going next door for a bite to eat. This was our first weekend being open and I have to finish up some paperwork but I can complete it when I get back."

I waited for Crystal in the lobby when she disappeared to the back area to inform the staff of her intensions. She was still the person I once loved and would die for. She still possessed beauty, brains, and a good sense of humor. Although I had to admit, while I stood there waiting, visions of her and Mr. Football flooded my memory banks. I figure I could at least let the past be just that. I could forgive but I was never going to forget.

When Crystal reappeared she was minus the doctor's lab coat and stethoscope. Her business skirt hugged her ass in all the right places with her blouse contoured perfectly to her upper torso and showing off her nicely shaped breasts. Of course, me being a shoe salesman, I noticed she had on a pair of Dolce & Gabbana business pumps. I had quickly forgotten how fine and jazzy she was but her attire reminded me with no problems.

We exited the building and made our way to the restaurant next door. While there we spent the next hour or so telling each other how our lives had progressed since college. Crystal hadn't missed a beat by graduating from the top percentile of her undergraduate class at USC then was accepted right into medical school there as well. After medical school, she completed her residency at Cedars-Sinai Hospital. Finally, three years later she opened her own medical practice in L.A. She said she opened a practice in South Central L.A. because she wanted to give back to the community that needed it the most. Now she was doing the same in Atlanta.

As for me, I told Crystal how my aspirations of making it to the major leagues fell way short due to my injuries while in college. I was amazed how she still knew my junior and senior year high school baseball stats when I led the state in four major categories. Crystal told me she taught I'd be winning a World Series with the Yankee's by now, but apparently that was a dream that didn't manifest. She even gave me support when I told her how everything turned out with Coca-Cola and I was now trying my hand at being an entrepreneur. Surprisingly, she even offered to help network for me in my field of marketing and even asked for the latest Cole Haan business pumps.

After we completed our meal, I gladly walked Crystal back to her office. We said our goodbyes but not before we exchanged cell numbers and promised to stay in touch. Crystal also mentioned she had just purchased a forty-five hundred square foot house off Cascade Road and still needed someone to show her around Atlanta. She even volunteered me as her personal tour guide for the next month or so.

As I maneuvered my car back onto I-285, headed towards Buckhead, it was almost six o'clock and I still had to meet with Diamond at her salon. The day was going pretty good so far as I made my quota, reconnected with Crystal, and now was about to find out more about my son. I noticed I had a few missed calls from crazy Nicole. She knew I was out making money but yet she continued to pester me whenever she got a chance. Raphael was more than likely back at my condo relaxing so I decided to give him a call instead.

"Hey boo boo," Raphael said as he answered his cell phone.

"What's up, man? What are you doing?" I asked.

"I'm just sipping on a glass of merlot and cooking dinner for us this evening," he replied.

"Who are us?" I asked.

"You, me and Nicole," he answered. "I decided to cook a light dinner before Nicole and I go out. Besides, she is eager to taste my signature Italian baked spaghetti with homemade garlic bread. Plus, I'm preparing a house salad made with fresh organic vegetable served with venerate dressing.

"So Nicole is coming to dinner?" I asked almost interrupting his last sentence.

"Yes darling and she has called me twice already asking if you were home yet," he replied.

"Well just between you and me, this conversation never happened," I exclaimed. "I have other things to worry about tonight and Nicole isn't one of them. Besides, I have other things to tend to before I come home."

"OMG, don't be so hard," he replied. "Nicole is sweet and just loves you Damien."

"Yeah, but there's a fine line between love and crazy. You two have fun tonight, I'll see you later."

"Okay lover boy, you do the same," he said. "Don't forget we have to be at the airport tomorrow for my flight."

"I won't. I got it covered, Raphael."

"Chow now," he said.

After I hung up with Raphael, I had made it to the downtown connector which was in mayhem. As expected there was heavy traffic so I hopped off the interstate and onto Peachtree Street downtown. It doesn't matter if it's Monday or Saturday you can always expect the traffic to be unpredictable in Atlanta. As I took the scenic route to Diamond's salon, I got a chance to soak in the beauty of downtown all the way up to the Buckhead district. It was hot and humid but people were still out sightseeing, going to various venues, and just having fun.

By the time I made it to Diamond's salon, it was a quarter past six. I figured Diamond was just finishing up as her salon usually closed early on Saturdays. I pulled into my less than conspicuous parking space with my BlackBerry in hand. I checked a few texts I received from clients earlier in the day. When I entered the salon, Tameka greeted me in her normal position behind the reception counter at the entrance.

"Hi Damien," she said. "I assume you are here to see Ms. Graham."

"Yes, that's correct," I replied.

"Well, she's in her office finishing up for the day but you can go ahead back there," she said. Just as I was about to turn and walk towards the back of the salon, Tameka asked me a question.

"Hey, is that the new BlackBerry phone you have in your hand?"

"It sure is."

"Can I see it?" she asked.

"Here you go," I said as I handed her the phone.

"So when you going to get me some boots?" she asked while fumbling with my phone.

"Boots," I exclaimed. "Girl its ninety-five degrees out there and you're asking for boots."

"Yes, Damien, I'm a boot freak and shop for them all year round. Especially this time of the year when their less expensive and right before the fall season."

"Okay, I see your point," I said. "Maybe I can check with my distributor later and let you know." As we finished our discussion, Diamond walks up out of nowhere and interrupts our conversation.

"Hello Damien, glad to see you could make it on time," Diamond said sarcastically while looking at Tameka.

"You know how this Atlanta traffic can be," was my response to her.

"Well Tameka, I'm leaving the salon early now as I have some matters to attend to," Diamond said. "I believe you and the remaining stylists can lock up when you're finished."

"Yes, Ms. Graham that should be no problem. We should be out of here in the next thirty minutes or so."

"That's fine," said Diamond. "I'll see you Tuesday morning, girl."

As Diamond and I were beginning to exit her salon, Tameka calls out to me regarding my phone. Apparently, I failed to retrieve it back from her.

"Hey Damien, here's your BlackBerry back," she yelled. "I'm sure you wouldn't want to forget this as it might come in handy."

"Oh thanks, Tameka, I almost forgot," I said grabbing my phone. "I definitely don't want to leave this."

Once outside the salon, I walked Diamond over to her car where she asked me to follow her to Sandy Springs where she owed a townhouse. We both got in our designated cars and I followed her down Piedmont Road until it merged onto Georgia 400. After going through the only toll the state of Georgia has, we continued to travel until reaching Northridge exit. As I followed her up the all brick three-level two door garage townhome, I noticed the plush green landscape and controlled gate access. These homes were easily price in the mid-three hundred thousand range, I thought to myself.

We both parked our cars in her garage and then made our way into the home.

Diamond gave me a brief tour of her home which was sleek and sophisticated to match her personality. Of course, she had a hint of pink décor throughout the house as well. After the tour, we retired to the living room on the second floor where she wanted to talk.

"Are you hungry, baby?" she asked walking to the kitchen. "I can make you something to eat."

"No, I'm still full from the late lunch I had," I replied as I made myself comfortable on her plush sofa.

When Diamond joined me on the sofa she had a glass of wine in one hand and Heineken in the other. It was perfect timing for the long day.

"Here you are Damien. I figured you would enjoy a cold one after a long day."

"Thank you, Diamond."

We both sat next to each other on the sofa sipping on our beverages while looking aimlessly into each other eyes. Then she got up and put on some smooth classic jazz so the mood would be right. When she returned to the sofa she had a photo album underneath her arm. She sat down next to me in almost the exact spot which she previously left.

"Well Damien, I'm glad you were able to meet me today because I want to show you some pictures of Christian."

As she began to open up the photo album, I took an unnoticeable deep breath as I didn't know what to expect. After that, I put the cold beer to my lips to quiche my thirst. The first picture I saw of Christian was a modern day photo. He had Diamond's color but the majority of my characteristics including height, wavy hair, and smile were very evident. Ironically, it was a picture of him in his baseball uniform proudly sporting his batting stance. I knew he was my son and began to crack a smile as Diamond noticed. Within the next hour, she showed me pages of Christian in various events and places. During this time, I got to know more about him as Diamond easily filled in the blanks for all the questions I had. I was able to see pictures of Diamond's mother and father who seemed to be well-respected people. Throughout the photo album, I noticed how everyone was always smiling and seemed to be having a great time. But there was one peculiar item I did notice in all the pictures. There was never a father figure captioned with Christian.

"Baby, I just want Christian to have a father in his life," Diamond said as we finished looking at the last photo. "And it's not about any money I'm coming after you for. As you see, I'm doing pretty well for myself."

"What do I say to a boy I haven't seen for almost ten years?" I asked. "I don't even know if he will be receptive to me."

"Damien, of course he has to get to know you," she stated. "But once he does he will love you. Besides, I have been telling him bits and pieces of who his father is hoping one day our paths would cross."

"So when is Christian coming down to Atlanta?" I asked.

"He'll be down here next month before school starts," she answered. "Since I moved down here at the beginning of the year, I wanted him to finish the school year in Chicago and enjoy the summer there with my parents.

"I don't know what to say, Diamond, because all this is so new to me."

"Just say you'll try, Damien."

"Ok sweetheart," I said. "We'll give it a go. Besides, I'm eager to see if he can hit a curve ball."

We laughed at my comment then hugged and kiss each other hoping the future would be bright for all of us. For the rest of the night we snuggled with each other, sipped on our drinks, and talked about Christian while listening to Diamond's vast jazz collection. When midnight came, Diamond and I curled up on the huge sofa under a soft wool blanket. The air conditioner was on full blast as we both held each other until falling asleep.

By 7:00 a.m., I awoke to the smell of coffee, bacon, and eggs with French toast. Diamond was definitely earning her brownie points with me for cooking breakfast. I didn't even know she possess the skill of cooking let along making breakfast. Within a few minutes I wolfed down my breakfast, kissed her goodbye, and was back on the interstate headed home. I had to have Raphael at the airport well before his noon flight back to Los Angeles. I hope he wasn't over indulged from partying the night before. I even figured once I got home and checked in on him I could get a quick catnap for myself.

When I arrived at my condo and walked through the front door I was startled and surprise. There in the middle of the kitchen was Raphael flipping pancakes like he was a gourmet chef. He was making ham and cheese omelets also.

"Hey boo boo," he shouted with excitement. "I was beginning to wonder if you were ever going to show up. Pull up a chair cause you made it just in time for breakfast. Oh and by the way please go wake up your part-time girlfriend, Nicole."

"I already had breakfast," I said. "What is Nicole doing here?"

"Honey, your girl was off the chain last night," he responded. "After a few shots of tequila, she got up on the bar and started to vogue in her Christian Louboutin's.

"What!" I yelled.

"Child all the gay guys loved her after that one," Raphael exclaimed. "I even had to drive us back home. Thank God she had a GPS in her car."

As I made my way back to my bedroom, there was Nicole underneath the covers as if she was freezing to death. The room smelled like a liquor refinery and I had to pinch my nose so the smell wouldn't kill me.

"Nicole," I said while shaking her. "Wake your drunk ass up, its Damien!"

"Damien, where the hell has your ass been all night?" she asked while still underneath the covers. "You didn't even come home last night and I wanted to surprise you." Without any hesitation she briefly peaked her head out from under the covers, looked at me, and went back to sleep.

I returned back to the kitchen where Raphael was now consuming his breakfast. I had to listen to him tell me how fabulous Club Bulldogs was and how he couldn't wait to return. Afterwards he cleaned the kitchen, washed the dishes, and placed Nicole's breakfast plate in the stove. I, on the other hand, took a long hot shower but not before I ordered Nicole to swallow a Goody's powder with ginger ale as she remained in my bed. Then Raphael and I bolted for the airport as I would deal with Nicole when I got back.

Chapter 26

It had been almost a month now, and Raphael was up to full speed at Diamond's salon. He had since packed up all his personal items in L.A. and placed them into storage. With a few suitcases of clothes he was now a resident of Atlanta with no intention of ever leaving. Raphael and I were quite comfortable in my centrally located condo. He went to work sometimes six days a week at Diamond's salon while I continued to hustle high end shoes, purses, and accessories for the ladies.

On this particular day it was Friday morning and payday for most people. The salon had a full schedule of clients and walk-ins as well. It was Katrina Hope's routine day to have her hair styled as usual. Katrina was a middle aged power woman who was classy, attractive, brash, and aggressive all rolled in one. This was probably why she didn't have a man since she thought she was always running the show. Katrina was a partner at the prestigious law firm McLaughlin, Hope, Berkowitz & Lee located in downtown Atlanta. Her firm handled high profile celebrity criminal cases and corporate civil claims. Katrina's motto was "if it doesn't make dollars it doesn't make sense," and she meant this with a passion. She was known exclusively for her high dollar clients who very often were acquitted or received huge settlements. As she walked into Diamond's salon, she wore a conservative, yet expensive, and stylist grey skirt suit with Prada heels and a matching bag. She walked with swag as her head peaked above her shoulders as if her shit didn't stink.

"Hello, Ms. Hope," said Tameka as she greeted Katrina coming through the salon doors from the receptionist desk. Tameka was always the first person patrons saw when they entered the salon. Her bubbling personality made them feel welcomed and it was an incentive which Diamond pushed for.

"How are you Tameka?" asked Katrina in a bougie tone as she looked around the salon. "I'm here for my scheduled nine o'clock appointment with Lance.

"Oh, Ms. Hope, I'm so sorry to inform you that Lance just called in sick about thirty minutes ago," exclaimed Tameka. He said he thought he could make it but apparently won't be able to.

"What!" shouted Katrina interrupting Tameka. "I cancelled my morning deposition in order to have my front lace weave styled on time and now this!"

"Yes ma'am, I'm so sorry to inconvenience you," said Tameka. "But we have twelve well qualified stylists here this morning. Any of whom can fit you into their schedules."

"Well that won't work," yelled Katrina. "I want my regular stylist, Lance, who is the only one I trust with my hair. Why didn't you notify me of this mishap before I drove all the way here from Alpharetta?"

"Ma'am I do apologize," responded Tameka as she flipped through the appointment log book trying to figure out a solution.

"Your salon has placed me in a precarious situation and now needs to accommodate and correct the problem," Katrina said with an attitude. Katrina's voice was beginning to resonate throughout the salon as customers began to notice.

One female customer sitting in a chair near the commotion whispered "Who does that bitch think she is?" Before Tameka or anyone could make a suggestion Raphael walked up to Katrina from behind and made a comment.

"Oh honey, where did you get those sexy peep-toe Prada pumps?" Raphael asked. "Those are to kill for and a must have, I definitely like." Unbeknownst to Katrina, Raphael had a shoe fetish and knew any and all designer shoe right on sight.

"Neiman Marcus," replied Katrina proudly but yet still hot and bothered. "And who are you to be asking?" she said eyeballing his six-foot four frame up and down.

"Child, I'm one of the best stylists up in here and damn good at it," responded Raphael. "I couldn't help but overhear all the commotion but would love for you to give me the opportunity to style your hair today."

"Well, if you know hair like you know shoes I should be okay," replied Katrina.

"I'm more than okay and you won't be disappointed, I promise," exclaimed Raphael while continuing to stroke Katrina's ego at the same time. Just like me, Raphael was a great salesman and marketer. "I just finished with a client a few moments ago, you can come sit in my chair right over here."

"Okay," she said in a suttle voice as she began to follow him.

As Raphael led Katrina away, he turned back and winked at Tameka as to say he had everything under control. Tameka simply smiled saying thank you with her facial expression.

Within the next two hours, Raphael and Katrina were all smiles and giggles like best friends. Raphael knew how to keep a conversation going and could influence the best of the best by his over the top flamboyant personality alone. It made him real and simply put people accepted it. Raphael had washed, conditioned, and placed Katrina under the blow dryer for a while. She was now back in his chair for the finishing style of weave.

"Well, you know Katrina my cousin has a great deal on high end shoes which I know you'll love to death."

"Oh no, I don't do bootleg," she replied while looking in the mirror in front of her as Raphael continued to style her hair.

"Darling, his shoes aren't bootleg," said Raphael. "There the real deal. He has the shoes before they hit Neiman Marcus. I thought maybe I could save you a few dollars."

"Really," she said. "These are real designer shoes not fake ones right?"

"Yes, they are the realist."

"Cause you know I can tell the fake from the real ones."

"Oh, I know your sophisticated self can tell the difference," he said. "Sweetie, I wouldn't even lead you down that road."

"Hope it doesn't sound too good to be true," said Katrina. "In any event here is my business card. Just have your cousin call me."

As Raphael continued to put the finishing touches on Katrina's hair there walked in a noticeable yet confident and older gentlemen. He seemed to be near sixty and had a simple appearance. He wore a pair of dark blue overalls, plaid shirt underneath, and dark workbooks were on his feet. He looked around the salon with thick black trim glasses he was wearing. To go along with his throwback fashion, he sported an almost shoulder length Jheri curl hairdo and a gold herringbone necklace. He looked around as if he was familiar with the salon but just was looking for someone in particular. Apparently, Tameka had briefly stepped away from her post and obviously couldn't help the gentleman.

"We'll look what the wind blew in," said Katrina as she took her eyes off the mirror in front of her to glance at the gentleman. "He definitely must be lost."

"Girl, the last time I saw a Jheri curl NWA was just breaking up in L.A.," replied Raphael. "And he looks a hot mess right about now."

The pair couldn't help but notice the gentleman as Raphael's salon chair was near the entrance door. Then as expected, the gentleman started walking towards Raphael with Katrina looking on.

"How ya'll doing?" asked the gentleman to Raphael and Katrina.

"Hello," said Raphael while Katrina act like the man didn't exist.

"Lookie here, my name is Odell," said the gentleman proudly in a Southern dialect. "Odell Montgomery to be exact and I'm from Willacoochee, Georgia. I'm here looking for a fella similar to yourself."

"Good heavens," shouted Raphael while Katrina remained silent. "Where on earth is Willacoochee, Georgia?"

"Boy, you must be from up the country somewhere," replied Odell. "You mean to tell me you don't know where Willacoochee, Georgia is?"

"No darling, I don't have the faintest clue," said Raphael. "I'm actually from Los Angeles and only been here in Atlanta for a short while."

"Oh, I sees it," said Odell while pushing up his glasses taking a better look at Raphael. "You from where all 'em young folks be killing each other over colors."

"Well, that was many years ago," answered Raphael with a chuckle. "It's really not like that anymore out there."

"My hometown is slow paced and about three hours south of Atlanta," said Odell. "Almost near the Florida state line in South Georgia."

"Oh my God, did you just say three hours?" asked Raphael.

"Sho nuff," replied the old-timer. "I've been driving long distances all my life and it ain't nothing. I use to be a truck driver for thirty five years before I retired a few years ago."

"What brings you into our salon Mr. Odell?" asked Raphael while continuing to style Katrina's hair.

"Well, like I mentioned earlier, the fella I'm looking for is similar to you," replied Odell. "He use to do my curl real good."

"Similar to me," exclaimed Raphael. "How so?"

"For starters he was tall and worked in this here salon," said Odell. "And he had them feminine ways bout him just like you."

"Feminine ways," stated Raphael as he paused styling Katrina's hair and placed one hand on his hip proudly while sticking out his chest. By now, Katrina was laughing silently and tried not to show it.

"Pay me no mind, son," said Odell. "I'm just describing him to you."

"I believe you're talking about Lance," said Raphael. "He's actually out of the salon today due to an illness."

"Yeah, yeah, yeah that's his name," yelled Odell. "My memory done got away from me over the last few years."

"Mr. Odell, I'd be more than glad enough to reprocess your Jheri curl. By the way, I'm Raphael. If you take a seat in our lounge area I should be finished with my client in about thirty minutes and can fit you in next.

"Thank you kindly, Raphael."

As Odell turned and was walking slowly towards the lounge area to take a seat, he was noticed by Tameka. She was returning to the front of the salon after retrieving some supplies from the back room.

"Mr. Odell is that you?" asked Tameka walking towards him.

"Hey Miss Lady, you still look good as ever." They both extended a hug to each other.

"So how you been doing since the last time I seen you?" asked Tameka.

"I've been good," replied Odell. "Just trying to maintain, baby doll."

"I don't see your wife here with you today. She didn't make the trip up here?"

"Naw, Ms. Hennrietta's arthritis in her toes been acting up lately. So she decided to stay at home and rest."

"Oh, I'm so sorry to hear that Mr. Odell. "Hopefully she'll get better soon."

"I recon she will. We got a big family reunion to go to next week in Chickasaw, Alabama. We gets to reunite with my daddy's folks and have a good time."

"Well, that sounds like a lot of fun. I'm sure Ms. Hennrietta will be fine by then."

"Lookie here Ms. Lady," said Odell pointing to his new work boots while slightly raising his right foot. "I got me a pair of new boots on today. I thought I'd see you in pair of them sexy long boots you usually wear."

"No, it's not quite cold enough for me to pull out my boot collection," she said laughing. "Besides I ordered a few new pairs and hopefully the next time I see you I'll have them on."

"Good enough." He casually smiled and then took his seat in the lounge area.

By now it was almost the lunch hour and the salon was packed with customers. They were getting the latest styles which always included weave or braids for the routine weekend in Atlanta. This included concerts, black-tie affairs, house parties, dates, and yes church. No woman in Atlanta went more than two weeks before she stepped back into a salon to get her weave styled. Otherwise, it was a sin and she stood out like a sore thumb.

Weaves were the trendiest styles in Atlanta since the invention of the flat iron. Chances were every woman you ran into had some form of weave in her hair. If she didn't, more than likely she wasn't from Atlanta. This tread started early for girls in junior high and progressed all the way to great-grandmothers and everything in between. Black woman and hair went together like peanut butter and jelly. If her bills weren't paid you could bet your last money her hair was laid. It was ritual, or better yet an obsession, for some to have their hair tight no matter what the cost. Besides, what better ways to attract a man than a fresh weave as if she was posing for *Essence Magazine*?

The salon was not only a place for obtaining the latest fashionable hair styles but an information center. It was a Mecca for gossip and a way to keep abreast of all the hottest news in and out of the community. If you heard a rumor in the salon, after a while it eventually came to light and was considered true. Every bit of news from politics, social media events, and even who was the next down low brother circulated in the salon. Everyone yearned for that juicy bit of gossip they could share with their co-workers, friends, and family.

Raphael had now completed Katrina's hair style and she looked fabulous. It only bolstered her conceited attitude as she stood out the chair and looked herself over from head to toe in the mirror. She touched her hair and smiled as Raphael took a lint brush and removed any remaining hairs from her jacket.

"Well, I must say Raphael, I am quite impressed. Seems like you just earned yourself a new client."

"Girl, it was nothing. Now you're all dolled up ready for that hot date this weekend."

"Hot date," she exclaimed. "I don't have time for that this weekend. Besides, I'm on my way into the office for a rescheduled deposition. Money before anything else!"

"Well, you know what they say about all work and no play, honey."

"Yes, Raphael, I know what they say. But right now I have to continue to get paid. My looks are one half of what keeps the opposition intimidated."

"So what's the other half?" asked Raphael.

"My brains," she professed.

Katrina gladly paid Raphael for the services he provided and tipped him with a fifty dollar bill. As she grabbed her purse, he offered to walk her to the door where they would say goodbye. As she began to walk out the door she made one more comment.

"Now don't forget to tell your cousin to call me," she said. "He can just come down to my firm and show me a few samples."

"Oh, I won't forget about you boo boo," he replied while holding the entrance door open for her. "By the way, his name is Damien."

"Okay, I'll await his call," she said while walking out the door. "See you in two weeks and thanks a million." Katrina promptly hopped in her grey convertible Bentley Continental GT and took off like rocket.

"Muuaahhh!" was his response as he fashioned his lips giving her a farewell kiss.

Once Katrina was out the parking lot Raphael began to walk towards the lounge area where Odell was waiting. He was approached by Tameka who watched Katrina depart from the salon.

"Hey Raphael, I just wanted to say thank you for helping me diffuse that situation with Ms. Hope. I'm on pins and needles every time she comes in here."

"Girl stop, don't even mention it! I'm use to dealing with women ten times that attitude and bank accounts to go along with it when I was in L.A. She just needs some attention and I'm not talking about hair."

"Oh, so you figured out why she was so uptight?" asked Tameka.

"Honey, women like that just need a good hard one to loosen their attitude up," he replied. "It's too bad she's not getting any with all that money she has."

Katrina laughed as she got the point of what he was referring to. Raphael had just made her day with that comment. Then she took her customary position at the entrance as more customers were beginning to trickle into the salon. Fortunate for her they all were nothing like Katrina.

Raphael then walked over to Odell who was patiently reading the morning edition of the Atlanta Journal Constitution. Among him were plenty of anxious women waiting for their stylist as well.

"Well, Mr. Odell, you ready to get your Jheri curl reconditioned?"

"Bout ready than I'll ever be."

"You can follow me back to my chair and we can get started. I'll have to see if I can find some Lustra Silk activator cream in here."

Chapter 27

The weekend was a blast. I made more money selling shoes and purses simply by referrals and word of mouth alone. It was all due to the product line I had and Mookie was the main person to thank for that. I could barely keep up with the orders constantly coming in let alone the women who were eager to buy every time I set foot in a different salon. By now, I was the man or at least that's what I thought. I was comfortable making tax-free dollars so easily but didn't want to get complacent as I couldn't hustle forever. Even if the hustle money continued to flow in, I eventually wanted to get into a routine of a normal nine to five or better yet start my legitimate business. By now, so many women knew me by face I felt like a celebrity.

Raphael being my temporary roommate was cool and had its perks. I felt like I was being pampered to death. For instance, every morning like clockwork he would prepare an enormous breakfast. And I'm not talking about some skimpy meal either. It was a full course meal which included scrambled eggs, sausage, bacon, pancakes or oatmeal, and French toast. Some days he would substitute the scrambled eggs with ham and cheese omelets with onions and green peppers. I felt like I was back in high school living in my grandmother's house again. Raphael told me he couldn't get his day started right unless he had his routine breakfast meal and by now I wasn't going to interfere with that.

Secondly, dinner in the evenings was the same but on a grand scale. After his shift at the salon was over, he would come home and prepare a healthy and hot meal. He cooked extravagant meals which included everything from chicken to lobster. Raphael loved to style hair but cooking was his passion. Simply put, the boy could cook his ass off.

I never keep my condo looking like a pigpen as I was considered clean and neat. But since Raphael had been living with me the place was spic-n-span all the time too. We were first cousins and I wasn't even charging him rent since I knew he would only be there a short while. Besides, I had so much money coming in from my hustle I didn't even need it. I guess Raphael felt compelled to cook and keep the place tidy while he lived there.

Eventually, being treated like a king in my own home would cease. Raphael was in the process of moving to a loft he found in midtown. It was just a matter of trying to decide which loft to pick as he had a few selections. After the negotiations, it would be a done deal.

It was now late Wednesday afternoon and I was driving to Katrina's law office downtown. Over the weekend, Raphael managed to tell me about this high-post woman who came into the salon demanding to have her hair styled immediately. He told me he later found out she was a high profile attorney who seemed to have a lot of disposable income. She also showed an interest in my inventory. That was just fine by me because I was addicted to money and wasn't going to turn down an opportunity to get paid. As we use to say in L.A. back in the day, "it seemed to be an easy lic." On Monday I called Katrina's office and surprisingly her receptionist was expecting my call. She told me to simply be at the office by 4:30 p.m. on Wednesday and not to be late.

As I maneuvered my whip downtown on Peachtree Street I noticed there was only fifteen minutes to spare before my meeting with Katrina. People with big money usually had big egos to go along with it, so I definitely didn't want to be late. My final destination was the thirty-five story Equitable Building. I was able to find a vacant parking space on Luckie Street right next to the building.

As I exited my car, I put a few quarters into the parking meter and grabbed the huge Saks Fifth Avenue shopping bag full of shoe boxes. I was able to look less suspicious and kept my business discreet. When I turned to walk up to the Equitable Building I notice a few homeless men across the street at Woodruff Park. I wanted to give them a few dollars, since I was blessed during the recession, but I was pressed for time. I figured I would follow up with them before my departure.

As I entered the building, it seemed as if everyone was heading for the exit. The long workday was over for most and now they were headed home but not before fighting that grueling Atlanta traffic. I walked over to the elevator and waited for the up button to light up. When it finally did, I jump on and headed upwards. Katrina's law firm had the entire thirty-fifth floor reserved for their company so I had quite a travel. When the elevator stopped I knew I reached my destination and proceeded to exit. I walked up to the enormous granite counter where a receptionist sat. Behind her was the lettering: McLaughlin, Hope, Berkowitz & Lee Law Firm. It was obvious I had reached my destination.

"Hello," I said walking up to the young female.

"Good afternoon, sir," she replied.

"I'm, Damien Hardy, here to see Ms. Katrina Hope."

"Yes, Ms. Hope is expecting you. Please have a seat and I'll let her know you have arrived."

It felt as if I was there for an interview or something while I waited noticing all the plush accommodations. But my casual attire which included a pair of khaki's and short sleeve button down was a dead giveaway. I didn't know what to expect as Raphael didn't go into any details of how Katrina looked but I did expect an attitude. When she did arrive in the waiting area, I knew it was her walking towards me. She was dressed in a pin-stripe navy blue skirt with the matching jacket and a pair of Alexander McQueen four-inch heels. Of course, I already knew she wore size seven by just glancing at her well pedicure feet. Katrina had to be pushing fifty but her aged was well concealed within her beauty. I knew this because her hips were spread and her breasts were cosmetically designed. She stood there brown skinned no more than five-foot seven. Her hair was still in tack as if Raphael just styled it thirty minutes ago. She was beautiful and attractive at a bare minimum.

"Hi, Mr. Hardy, I'm Ms. Hope," she said while extending her hand.

"Hello, Ms. Hope," I said quickly standing up embracing my hand to meet hers.

"Now, that we've met, let's not be so formal. I'll call you Damien and you can call me Katrina."

"That works for me."

Instantly, I knew she had that take charge mentality and always wanted to be in control. At this point, I really didn't care. I'd let her be the man as long as I got paid. All I wanted to do was show her my inventory and get out of there as the whole law firm ambiance was making me nervous.

"Ah, I see you brought me some goodies," she said looking down at my shopping bag.

"Yes, I did," I replied. "And I made sure to bring plenty of size sevens."

"How did you know I wear size seven?"

"Well, let's just say you know law and I know shoes." Katrina didn't know more than half of my clients wore size seven as it was a very popular size among women. To be safe, I even brought a few size eights.

"I like that one Damien," she said smiling. "Let's move into my office were we can have a bit of more privacy."

I grabbed my oversized shopping bag which was actually obtained from Nicole who loved to shop at Saks. As Katrina led the way back to her office, I watched her ass swayed from side to side and nearly got a full hard on. Her skirt was tight enough to make me fantasize but like always I kept my composure. I dealt with a lot of women on a daily basis and I always remembered to simply keep it professional as it kept the money flowing. Besides, if any of my clients wanted to get with me, I always took the laid back approach and let them make the first move. When we arrived at Katrina's office it was roomy and well put together as I would have thought. The view from at the top floor was one to die for. If I had a view like that I would make the office my home as well. Once inside, she closed the door so we could get down to business. Since she was a high end potential client, I brought the best product to fit her profession. This included Christian Louboutin, Prada, and Gucci to name a few. I felt like a salesman at Macy's again. One by one she tried on eight of the eleven pair of shoes I brought and was overwhelmed with excitement. I never over saturated a client with too many top designer shoes. Keeping it limited to a selected few made their selections short and simply. Otherwise, women would take all day to buy one pair.

"Damien, I'm just too impressed. Your cousin was right, I feel like I'm actually at Neiman's trying to decide.

"So buy them all," I said jokingly.

"You know what, I will just do that."

And just like that Katrina purchased all eight pair of shoes she tried on. She didn't buy the remaining three because they were size eight and too big. Her total came to right around fifteen hundred dollars and she didn't even blink twice. You have "to know taste to know taste" fit the occasion. Katrina knew my products were original high end shoes from the vendor and she wasn't passing up a great deal. Besides, what she bought from me would cost her well over three grand in the mall or boutiques in Atlanta. Even though she had the money, everyone needs a bargain sometimes to feel special.

"Damn Damien, I feel like the luckiest women in Atlanta right now."

"You should feel like that. I just gave you a sweet deal."

"Let's say you and I celebrate at Bones. Are you familiar with the place?"

"Yeah, it's on Piedmont Road."

"Correct and besides I could use a stiff drink to go along with the hectic week it's already been. On the way there I can stop by my bank's ATM and get the cash I owe you.

"That's sounds good, I'm all in."

Bones restaurant was an establishment frequented by the movers and shakers and not for the ordinary people of Atlanta. Well, at least that was the perception of many people in Atlanta. Most of the patrons included high profile celebrities and sport figures. I figured Katrina tied up quite a few high end deals over cocktails with her colleagues there.

"I'll call the matradee and have him reserve my normal table there," she said. "Oh by the way, you'll need a jacket to enter. Do you wear a forty-two regular?"

"No, I'm actually a forty-four," I replied.

"Fine, I'll make sure the matradee has your jacket available once we arrive."

Within a few minutes, we both were departing her office headed for the elevator. The receptionist had since left as it was now almost six o'clock and well into the rush hour in Atlanta. Katrina agreed to pull her car around where I parked on Luckie Street so I could place the shoes in her car. Then I would follow her to the ATM and restaurant.

When we arrived at Bones, Katrina was well greeted beginning with the valet staff. Everyone seemed to really know her and extended a more than friendly welcome. Once inside the matradee had a sporty navy blue blazer awaiting me. He even assisted me with putting it on, and then we were promptly seated. For once, I felt like a male groupie or a kept man with Katrina by my side. Once at our table Katrina, ordered a cosmopolitan and I had a Heineken that was brought to me in a glass. She felt compelled to make a recommendation from the menu as I had never eaten at the establishment before. She ordered a crab stuffed trout while I settled for the bone-in rib eye. Within the next few hours we both were stuff and I could tell she had a buzz from her second drink. Our eyes met like they never did before and I knew it was on.

"It's getting a bit stuffy in here," said Katrina. "Let's go back over to my place so we can relax more."

"That's cool with me," I replied. "So where do you live?"

"Not too far from here in Alpharetta."

"Okay, I'll follow you."

Who was I fooling as if where she lived really mattered? I would have followed her to Tennessee if I knew I was going to get some pussy. By now, Katrina was looking at me as if she was a cougar and I was her prized cub for the night. We exited the restaurant then retained our designated vehicles from the valet.

Like previously, I followed right behind her in my car. After we traveled north on Georgia 400, for about ten minutes, we finally exited off Haynes Bridge Road. After that we made a few turns and I was completely lost as I had never been on that side of Atlanta before. We finally arrived at a plush gated community where a security guard was positioned at the entrance. I noticed the sign which read: County Club of the South. Katrina pulled up to the guard where I heard her tell him I was her guest for the evening. He then motioned for me to simply follow her into the community.

When we pulled up to her house it had to be at least five thousand square feet in size. Plus, her home came equipped with a three door garage. She pulled into one to the garages as the door rolled up. I parked my car on the outside and walked into the garage before the door came down. We entered her home from the garage and ended up in the kitchen.

Once inside, we both went at it with no hesitation. Our lips met as we kissed each other then I grabbed the back of her hair. Her head went back as she let out a pleasurable moan and I kissed her neck. Simultaneously, I slid my other hand under her blouse and unstrapped her bra smoothly. While I kissed her breasts she slid her skirt down and kicked off her heels. Not to my surprise she had no panties on. Then she unzipped and pulled down my pants. While my pants were around my ankles she violently ripped off my shirt.

"Damien, are you ready to fuck this pussy?"

"Only if you promise to give it to me right."

"I promise."

After our short exchange of words, I lifted her up on the kitchen island with her legs extended in the air and placed my hard dick inside her. Her pussy was juicy wet, but tight at the same token. I knew she was overdue and needed a more than routine workout.

"Oh yes, Damien!" she screamed and giggled at the same time while I stroked her going deeper every time. "You like this seasoned pussy?"

"Hell yeah," I replied. "I like this seasoned pussy. It's real tight and wet just like I like it."

"Well, then show me and fuck me like you do!"

At that point, I grabbed her ass off the island and fully extended her on my erect dick as her legs wrapped around my arms. There I was standing in the middle of her kitchen while she rode my dick as I stood straight up. Katrina continued to scream and moan as I looked into her face but her eyes where closed from the pleasure. All those years in the weight room paid off and knowing how to leverage my body kept her properly on my dick as I lifted her up and down so effortlessly.

"Yes Damien, stroke that seasoned pussy like you want it! Your dick is so hard and thick, give it to me boy."

It was obvious Katrina was a talker and quite good at it while having sex. All the trash talking was actually turning me on as she knew how to finesse a man's ego. I quickly placed her back on the island. As I motioned for her to turn around she quickly latched on my dick with her mouth. While she continued to suck my dick, I made her spit on it so it would be good and wet when I entered her again. Then I spun her around on the island and fucked her doggy style.

"Awwwhhh, you going to make mama's pussy come like that boy!"

"That's what I'm supposed to do damnit! Now show me what you working with and go to work on that dick."

I pulled her hair back with both hands while she was positioned on her hands and knees. Katrina screamed even more and I knew she liked it. She knew just exactly what I wanted as she stroked her ass back and forth on my dick and I stood watching making her do all the work. I continued to stroke her at this position for a while. Then just as she was beginning to climax I stopped and made her get on top as I lay on the island. Before though, she removed my pants which we still around my ankles. Eventually, she came screaming telling me which was a dead giveaway. I came thereafter knowing she had been satisfied. In a few minutes, we ended up moving upstairs to her bedroom where we repeated the process then fell asleep. It was well deserved and earned by both of us.

Katrina was the veteran Mookie warned me about. Her actions in the kitchen and bedroom warranted her that prized distinction. But I knew Katrina was a power struggle and always wanted to be in control, even in sex. So that told me early on we were surely going to bump heads later on down the line if our sexual encounters were to continue. Woman of her caliber never wanted to give the upper hand to a man. For some apparent reason it made them feel as if they were not truly independent of one. I couldn't be mad at her for that, because at the end of the night we both got what we wanted out the deal.

Before the sun came up so did we both again. Then I put my clothes back on, input my address into my car's GPS, and headed home. For Katrina, it was sure enough going to be another hectic day at the office. Well, at least she was able to relieve all that built up stress from the night before.

Chapter 28

It was almost 11:30 a.m. on Sunday morning as I circled the block trying to find a parking spot at Atlantic Station. Crystal had agreed to meet me there for an early lunch on her only day off. I figured it would it would be a good time for us to talk as I knew deep down inside I still had feelings for her. Who was I fooling? She was my first love and I guess those feelings were hard to let go, even after all those long years. I even had a sexy pair of red Cole Haan business pumps for her and a purse to match.

"C'mon man," I screamed out loud. "You mean to tell me there's not a parking spot on this block." By now, I was going in circles trying to find a parking spot rather than park in the garage. If I parked there I would have to walk farther. Finally, I drove up to a burgundy Chevy Tahoe and saw its reverse lights come on. I patiently stopped and waited for the SUV to pull forward out of the spot I wanted. When it did, I zipped my bimmer quickly into the spot it once occupied. Then I inserted a handful of quarters into the parking meter and headed towards the quad where we agreed to meet. Once there Crystal and I could decide which restaurant to select.

As I walked on the sidewalk, I turned the corner and came upon the opening to the quad. I noticed Crystal sitting on a bench with a sexy sun dress on. Her legs were crossed and she had a nice pair of sandals on to show off her fresh pedicure. Her back was slightly towards me and obviously she could not see me even with her shades on. Within a few moments, I walked up to her and touched her shoulder.

"Hello beautiful," glad to see you could make it."

"Hi Damien," she said turning around, and then stood up. She gave me a big hug with a kiss on my right cheek.

"Sorry to keep you waiting but it took me forever to find a parking spot."

"Oh, don't worry about it. I actually just sat down a few minutes ago and was enjoying the view and sun."

"So did you have a place in mind to eat?" I asked.

"It doesn't matter to me, Damien. I'll defer to you since you know more about Atlanta than I do."

"You cool with Fox Sports Grill?"

"Yeah, that's fine, I heard about that place," she replied. "Just lead the way. We probably can watch the Braves who are set to play today at noon."

That's what I liked most about Crystal. Even back in the day she was all girly girl but could sit down with you and partake in a sports game and actually know what's going on. She wasn't like some of the women I went out with, all glamorous without a slightest clue between a football or baseball game.

"Well, you know they have a few pool tables in there," I said as we began to walk. "I was thinking after our lunch I could whip you up in a friendly game of pool."

"No sir, Mr. Hardy. If anyone is going to take an ass whipping today it's definitely you. Do you remember how I use to beat you all the time in pool and bowling back in the day?"

"No, I don't really remember that."

"Well, look who has caught amnesia now," she said and we both laughed.

"Just don't get too cocky," I replied. "You know there's a bowling alley around here too. I'll have to make you eat those words."

"I'm game if you are, baby. Don't let the PHD fool you, I still got game."

Crystal still had that competitive attitude just like before and was comical about it. Even in high school we managed to push each other to the limit in everything so we could succeed. It was always friendly competition but yet we made it fun.

We continued to joke and casually talk until we reached the entrance of the establishment. Our hostess sat us immediately and I was glad because my stomach was growling like a little tiger. Crystal ordered a Caesar salad with grilled shrimp and I had my usual hungry man meal which included a twelve-ounce T-bone steak, oversized baked potato loaded with butter, and a house salad. I also ordered a water and ginger ale to wash it all down.

"You ready to take that ass whipping now?" I asked after we ate.

"No, the question is are you ready to take your ass whipping?" she responded.

"Crystal, let's make a friendly wager just like back in the day."

"Back in the day we both were broke so we couldn't wager anything. So what did you have in mind?"

"If I win you owe me another date," I said.

"Okay, that's fair," she replied. "And if I win you owe me three pair of shoes, of my choice, and the purses to match."

"Damn, that's a pretty high wager!"

"What's the matter, you scared?" Crystal asked.

"Hell no, you got yourself a bet." We both shook hands right there and proceeded to move to the area where the pool tables were.

During our first game of pool, I easily prevailed against Crystal. She was a little rusty as she still had three balls on the table when I knocked the eight ball in. I thought for a minute it could have been a strategy move on her part but I didn't care as I was out to win. Before the first game we agreed to play the best two out of three series. Now, all I had to do was win the second game but Crystal wasn't having that. On our second game she beat me pretty convincingly, so I had to make sure I won the final one. Just as I had imagined game three was a slug fest. By then, we both had our rhythm well into swing and whoever made a mistake could cost them the game. The game was down to the eight ball being knocked in and it was Crystal's turn.

"So how bad do you want those designer shoes?" I asked.

"Real bad, Damien, just watch and see me hit this eight ball in."

"Where are you going with it?" I asked. "You know you have to call a pocket."

"Eight ball all the way down in the left corner pocket," she stated.

Crystal was attempting to make a difficult shot by hitting the eight ball off the upper side of the pool table and hoping the ball would travel all the way across the table to the pocket she called. Even for a professional, the shot was difficult. It was all or nothing because she knew if she missed I would have a clear easy shot for the win. We both were risk takers since high school and now wasn't any different.

When she struck the eight ball I held my breath for a moment knowing I hated losing at anything. The connection from the cue ball was perfect and solid as we both watched the eight ball bounce against the table's edge and towards the winning pocket. The ball missed the pocket by an inch and bounced back into the center of the table.

"Looks like no designer shoes for you."

"Darn it, Damien, you jinx me with all you're talking."

"Oh no, no, no. Don't even try that lame excuse. Eight ball in the right side corner pocket for the win," I exclaimed. After I hit the eight ball it disappeared into the corner pocket as I called it. "Looks like somebody owes me another date."

"I let you win and you know it," she said then smiled. "There was no way I should have tried to make that difficult shot."

"Excuses, excuses, excuses," I replied.

By now, more than three hours had elapsed since we first walked through the front door. We decided to call it an end to our lunch date. As we left I decided to walk Crystal back to her car and we continued to converse. Crystal stopped in front of a white Mercedes Benz S550 with light smoke tinted windows.

"Well, here we are," she said.

"So I see you have my dream car," I said. "Your Benz is really nice."

"Thank you, Damien, but I figured your dream car would be a Lamborghini or Ferrari."

"It would be if I was playing in the majors."

"You want to take my car for a spin around Atlanta now?" she asked.

"Maybe later, I'm cool just sitting in it for now," I replied.

Crystal placed her hand on the driver's side door handle and the remaining doors unlocked. She sat down and turned on the air conditioner while I made myself comfortable on the passenger's side. It must have been recently purchased because it still had the new car smell.

"So what happened to you and I Crystal?" This was the first time we ever talked about the horrific event back in '93. "Why did I have to catch you with that guy?"

"Damien, I was young and naïve back then and got caught up in a lot of nonsense."

"Nonsense like what? Did he sell you a dream with his NFL ambitions?"

"We had a class together and he was dominating and caring like you but you weren't around. I know I can't justify cheating on you, but I really am sorry. After the incident, I tried to reach you so many times but you evaded my calls. Later, I found out you enrolled at the University of Miami to play baseball."

"After fifteen years, I forgave you a long time ago Crystal but I just haven't forgotten. You see a man must learn to forgive in order to move on in the future."

"And I don't expect you to forget," she said. "But I do want you to let me make amends for the past and put our relationship back on track the way it use to be or even better."

"I don't know, Crystal. So much has changed and is different now."

"Do you believe in fate or destiny?" she asked.

"Why do you ask?"

"Why it is after all these years our paths have crossed again in Atlanta?" she asked.

"I never really gave it any thought."

"It's because it was meant to be Damien. Baby, after all these years I still love you and want us to put our lives back together with each other in it. I want to be exclusively with you, I promise. Everyone deserves a second chance."

Crystal was bringing a lot of heat on me at that moment. It was already nearly one hundred degrees outside but our conversation was hotter. I still loved her but didn't quite yet know how to convey it to her as my pride got in the way. I thought about Christian and knew I had to tell her about him.

"Crystal, there's something I must tell you."

"What is it Damien?"

"I have a son that's almost nine, named Christian. He lives in Chicago now but will be moving here next week to Atlanta and live with his mother."

"I think that's wonderful you're a part in his life," she said. I'm willing to give you all the support you need with him that his mother will allow."

"There's no baby mama drama if that's what you mean. It's all new to me Crystal. I didn't even know about him until this summer."

"Well, you're a father in your son's life and that what counts. Regardless, you're stepping up to the plate and being responsible like always and I love you for that."

Crystal always knew how to make me feel at ease and confident at the same time. She didn't look at my situation as negative but as a building and bonding experience for all. As time progressed she decided to drive me to my car so we could say our goodbyes until we met again. The ride in her Mercedes was smooth and I knew shortly we would have to exchange cars for a day or so. She finally pulled up to where I parked.

"You sure you're not on the Yankee's roster?" she asked. "That's a nice ride you have yourself."

"Yes, I'm positive," I said laughing. "Thanks for the compliment on my car but its older than it looks. You'd be surprised how much a consistent wash and wax goes.

Before she drove off, I reached into the back seat of my car and gave Crystal the shoes she asked for. The purse was icing on the cake as she loved them both and gave me a kiss.

"I'll see you later, Damien," she yelled while slowly pulling off with her passenger side window slightly down. "Once again, thanks for the shoes, love ya!"

"So when will I see you again?" I asked.

"Real soon, I promise. Remember, I still owe you a date."

Chapter 29

The next day I received a call from Mookie stating he wanted me to come by so I could restock my inventory. Apparently, he had just received another shipment and was planning to distribute the products to his wholesalers. I found it kind of odd because I usually initiated a call to him when my inventory was low or if I needed a specific item. I figured he was staying ahead of all orders by simply being proactive.

The additional inventory would come in handy as Nicole had set up another shoe and purse party at her girlfriend's house for the weekend. I had told her I would easily get her the products to her before then. Besides that, I had tried to distance myself from her to no avail. Trying to be all business and no pleasure with Nicole wasn't as simple as you might think. She still expected our relationship to be the same as if I never left Coca-Cola. Every day I would try to think of how I could wash my hands free and clean of her. But as long as she was still helping me sell products it wasn't going to be an easy task. Deep down inside I knew the only way I could remove myself from her was to stop this whole business entity we had developed. For now, it wasn't an option.

I arrived at Mookie's house when the afternoon heat was mostly intense during the day. I couldn't wait for the fall season to arrive so the temperature would subside. Until then there was no end in sight for the heat madness that seemed to plague the city all day long. As I pulled into the driveway, I noticed his mom's car was gone. She was at work and we wouldn't have to be so discreet with the products. I sat in my car an extra minute with the air conditioner on high. Even though Mookie's front door was only a few feet away, I dreaded going out in the heat and humidity.

"Is it hot enough out there for you?" asked Mookie while opening the front door just as I was walking up. "I saw you pulling in the driveway a few minutes ago. Come on in out the heat."

"What's up, man?" I asked as we gave each other our customary dap and hug. "You, been alright?"

"Yeah, I've been good, I really can't complain."

"Same here Mookie."

Mookie led me to the basement where he kept his inventory stashed and out of sight of his mom's view. At this point, she didn't even know what he had going on and he planned to keep it that way for now. Before we went down into the basement we stopped in the kitchen where he fixed himself a tall glass of ice tea and offered me a lemon lime Gatorade out the refrigerator. By the time we got to the basement, he already had the inventory laid out ready for me to make my visual selections. For the next ten minutes, I selected items while he marked them off his makeshift inventory sheet.

"Damien, let me ask you something."

"Shoot bro."

"You ever think about your future and what's your purpose in life?"

"All the time, Mookie, especially now. Why do you ask?"

"I've been thinking a lot lately about us hustling these products."

"Yeah, what about it," I said still inspecting and picking out my items.

"Well, you know we can't hustle forever, right?"

"I agree with you on that one man. But I guess just like everything in life this is temporary until something changes."

"That's right, but how do you know for how long something is temporary and what constitute a change?"

"Ok Mookie, what's up with the philosophy lecture?"

"What I'm trying to say is that my days hustling these products are about to come to an end."

"So what brought about that?" I asked.

"Her name is Nadine."

"Nadine? That sounds like someone's grandmother."

"Very funny Damien," said Mookie laughing. "But we're actually the same age. We met last month at the party my mom had for me here."

"So what's the scoop on her?" I asked.

"She an intelligent woman who understands me and knows all about my past. She accepts me without being judgmental."

"Well, I can't knock her for that. Just as long as your happy."

"What I'm trying to say, Damien, is that she's different, man. She even got me to look at my accident in a different perspective, saying it was a purpose to all of it. She taught me my failures could be someone else's gain in life by sharing my story."

"Damn that's deep," I said. I never really looked at it like that before."

"Real talk, bro. Nadine even got me a job as a mentor advisor at the Boys and Girls Club in downtown Decatur. A forty hour a week job with full benefits. She knew the hiring manager and all."

"Hey man, that's cool Mookie! I'm really happy for you."

"That's cooler than a fan on a hot August day in the A-T-L," he said. "Can you imagine that? I was busting my ass trying to find a job after coming out the joint and always came up slap empty until I met her. I guess it is all about who you know."

"So what will you be doing at the Boys and Girls Club?"

"I'll be working with a mentorship program and high risk youth programs. Basically, I try to keep kids out of trouble and stay free and clear of the path I took in life. The organization felt I had a real life testimony that could hit home with the kids."

At that moment, I knew Mookie was really happy with himself for the first time in a while. Back in our college days at Miami he used to drink as if he was running away from his problems. Now, he was facing them head on, accepting them like a man. We both stopped overlooking the inventory on the basement floor and I gave him a congratulatory hug. For once, I knew Mookie was going to be alright.

"I'm amped up, man," he said. "For once in my life I feel like I'm serving a greater purpose other than myself. When I first went to prison I was so bitter trying to figure out why things turned out they way they did. Prison will humble you quickly, especially when you find out it's full of people with broken promises."

"I guess in order to be a testimony to others you have to go through your own test in life."

"I couldn't have agreed with you more," he replied. "So once this inventory is gone than so am I, out of this racket. I'm pulling out of this one while I'm ahead of the game."

"Ironically, I've been thinking about letting this hustle go myself Mookie. Over the summer I saved a lot of money and now can really start my own legitimate business."

"So what did you have in mind?"

"I thought about my own marketing consulting business. Since I already deal with a huge number of female clients who either own their own business or work for a major company, I could solicit my services through them. I'd help clients better their business by exposing marketing techniques that allow them to thrive and generate more income."

"That's a great idea, Damien. I knew it was only a matter of time before you figured a way to flip your hustle into your advantage. You always were the smart entrepreneur type in college."

"Yeah, like Nadine said there's a purpose to everything in life, but you got to use it to your advantage. Even Coca-Cola letting me go after all these years, it was just what I needed to start my own thing."

"Good riddance to those clowns," he said. "That's their lost and your gain. Plus, you're too smart to be working for anyone else. But answer this last question for me?"

"Shoot, what is it?" I asked beginning to rumble through the inventory one last time.

"I know you're not going to let your starting five go!" he said.

Instantly, I stopped in my tracks and looked at Mookie. We both burst out laughing remembering how long ago he had explained the whole "starting five concept" to me in college. It was comical but yet so true. Atlanta was still a haven where any man with a little bit of game could have a roster full of desperate women and Mookie always knew that.

We spent the next few hours reminiscing and laughing about our old college days but knew our latter days ahead would be better than our former. At this point in time it seemed like things were changing so quickly and for the best. Someone once said, "A man changes many times, but a fool remains the same." I really knew what that meant now as we both would always be a work in progress in order to better ourselves.

After I selected my inventory for what seemed to be the final time, I brought Mookie up to date on my situation with Diamond. He was more than supportive, saying he wished he even had a son to watch grow up. Maybe that wasn't too far off in the near future for him.

When the evening rush hour commenced, I was headed out of Mookie's house. I didn't mind being stuck in traffic headed home as I would be happy thinking about all that had transpired for the day. My best friend was happy, full of life, and making a positive change. And for once, so was I.

Chapter 30

The day had finally arrived when I would meet my son, Christian. Diamond had flown back to Chicago the week before and had arrived back in town yesterday with Christian by her side. School was set to start in less than a week, but Diamond had already gotten Christian's paperwork all taken care of. She had enrolled him in a charter school near her home. The school was known for excelling in math, reading and competency scores.

I was nervous as hell while I drove north on Georgia 400 headed to Diamond's home. Even though my car's air condition was blasting on high, I still was sweating. What would I first say to him? How receptive would he be towards me? These were the questions I kept asking myself over and over again while driving. I tried to tell myself everything was going to be just fine but the anxiety was eating me up inside. My nervousness intensified when I turned off the exit leading to Diamond's home and I knew it was no turning back now.

As I drove up to the gated security entrance, I pressed the numbers nine, five, and eight with the pound sign following thereafter on the keypad. This was the gate code Diamond had given me earlier. Then I waited for her sweet voice through the intercom system.

"Hello."

"Hey Diamond, it's Damien. I'm at the gate right now."

"Hi baby, I'll buzz you in. Just drive to my garage which will be open and park inside. Christian and I will be upstairs."

"Okay, see you in a few minutes."

Once inside the gate, I drove around a curve and onto Diamond's townhome. The atmosphere was just as I saw it before. It was quiet, peaceful, and the landscape was very well cared for. When I pulled up to Diamond's townhome, she had one of her garage unit's door already up as she mentioned. After I pulled inside the motion sensor triggered the door to close behind my car.

As I exited my car, I grabbed the gift bag from my back seat. Since Christian was an avid baseball fan I picked him up a bat and a professional leather glove. I even had a few autographed baseballs from the Los Angeles Dodges to go along with the surprise. I figured the items would be a good ice breaker with us. I took one final deep breath and proceeded to enter the home from the garage.

I walked up a flight of stairs and entered the kitchen on the second floor where Diamond was waiting for me. I smelled the aroma of Sunday dinner cooking. The air was filled with the scent of pot roast, canned yams, macaroni and cheese, and fresh steamed vegetables. I had to do a double take and make sure I was in the right place.

"Hi baby," said Diamond as she hugged me. "Glad you could make it."

"You got it smelling like a café up in here," I said. "I didn't know you could burn like that."

"I'm doing a little something. Besides, I didn't learn to cook overnight, my mom taught me most of what I know."

"So where's Christian?"

"He's in the living room watching the Braves vs. Cubs game on TV. C'mon, I'll introduce you to him."

With my gift bag in tow, I followed Diamond through the kitchen into the living room area. When we arrived in the living room, Christian was sitting directly on the carpeted floor Indian style with all eyes on the fifty-inch TV screen in front of him. Sitting with his back towards us, I didn't even think he heard us approaching.

"Christian, can you please come here for a minute? I want you to meet someone."

"Yes ma'am."

Christian stood up still looking at the TV screen then turned around towards us. He was slightly tall for a soon to be nine year old and was wearing a Chicago Cubs baseball cap with pride. I saw myself in him as his frame replicated mine when I was his age. Within a few seconds he was in front of us.

"Christian, this is Damien," she said. "Damien, this is Christian."

"Hi Mr. Damien, it's nice to meet you."

"Well, it's nice to meet you Christian," I said.

He extended his hand to me and we both shook while I smiled at his politeness. The nervousness left me altogether. He seemed to be well mannered and articulate for such a young kid, something you rarely see in kids nowadays.

"So what's in the bag?" he asked.

"Well, your mom told me you were a big time baseball fan. So, I got you a bat, glove, and a few baseballs autographed by the Dodgers."

"Wow! The Los Angeles Dodgers."

Christian quickly grabbed the bag as I extended it towards him. He tore through the color tissue paper searching for the baseballs. I was able to call in a favor to Coach Frazier last week who still kept in contact with the staff and management for the Dodgers. He was more than happy to get a few baseballs autographed and overnight them to me once I told him my situation. By now, Diamond and I were smiling at each other.

"Look mom," he said with excitement holding up the baseballs he found in the bag. "I have two autographed baseballs from the Dodgers."

"I see Christian, now what are you suppose to say."

"Thank you, Mr. Damien," he said.

"Oh, don't mention it Christian. It was no big deal."

All three of us moved into the living room where Diamond and I sat on the sofa next to each other. Meanwhile, Christian assumed his position in front of the TV and had located the bat and glove within the bag by now. He stood in front of the TV with the bat in his hand duplicating his hitter's stance.

"Be careful, Christian," Diamond exclaimed. "Make sure you don't hit the TV."

"Don't worry, I won't mom."

Then just as excited as he was with the baseballs and bat, he turned his attention to the glove. He tried it on and mimicked catching a fly ball and throwing it back to home plate to prevent a scoring run. The glove fit him perfectly as he turned his attention back to me.

"Hey, I know who you are," he said to me.

"You do?" I replied.

"Yes, you're the man in the pictures my mom has been showing me."

I thought to myself Diamond must have showed him our pictures from back in the day when I first met her. Or maybe the most recent pictures we took of ourselves since we reconnected.

"Yeah, I guess you're right Christian."

"You played baseball at the University of Miami, right?"

"Yes, I sure did."

"Well, I'm going straight to the majors when I finish high school."

"Whoa, now hold your horses All-Star," I said laughing. "What about college first? You got to have something to fall back on in life like an education if baseball doesn't work out."

"Oh, I see your point Mr. Damien. I guess if I had to go to college, I'd pick the University of Southern California."

"USC!" I yelled in excitement. "What do you know about their program?"

"Well, they won twelve College Baseball National Championships, had twenty-one College World Series appearances and thirty-six NCAA Tournament appearances. All of which are still records to this day. Even though my baseball idol didn't play his college ball there I would still attend."

"Who's your baseball idol?"

"Barry Bonds," he said smiling. "You do know who that is right?"

"Yes, All-Star I know who Barry Bonds is," I replied while smiling back at Christian.

It was evident Christian was witty, smart, and had amassed a wealth of baseball knowledge. I was in awed wondering how a kid could have such an insight but I loved it. Since he was a baseball fanatic we would get along just fine.

"Let's say you and I go outside in the back yard," I commented. "I want to see if you can hit a curve ball."

"I'm pretty sure I can, Mr. Damien," he replied. "I was the MVP on my summer league baseball team back in Chicago."

He had the confidence and a hint of brashness which I liked. It reminded me of myself when I was his age. I couldn't be mad at him though, you needed a little bit of that in order to succeed in life anyway.

"But first you have to ask your mom for permission to go outside."

By now, Diamond had made her way back into the kitchen finishing up Sunday dinner. She also wanted us to bond and have a few moments to ourselves.

"Mom, can I please go outside in the back yard and play ball with Mr. Damien?" he yelled from the living room.

"Yes, that should be fine," she said walking over towards us smiling. She knew we were bonding and wasn't going to interfere with that. "Besides, dinner won't be ready for another thirty minutes or so."

"Alright! C'mon Dr. Damien," he said while grabbing the baseballs, glove, and bat all at the same time. "Last one to the back in a rotten egg."

Diamond and I continued smiling and hugged each other as Christian made a dash for the back yard. We both knew everything was going to work out just fine.

Chapter 31

When I left Diamond's house it was almost nine o'clock. The sun's horizon could barely be seen in the summer sky as I traveled back towards Buckhead. I was very pleased Christian and I had bonded so well together. Diamond was so excited she asked me to join her by taking Christian to school next Monday. It was going to be the first day of school for all students in Fulton County and I agreed without hesitation.

The whole DNA situation still concerned me as I felt guilty with the thoughts. I knew by Christian's traits he was my son but there was another side to me saying get the proof in writing. I thought back and forth on whether to mention the DNA test to Diamond and how she would respond. The last thing I wanted to do was rock the boat and imply I didn't trust her. Like anything else, I decide to sleep on it for a while and revisit the idea later.

I was still a few miles from my condo when I retrieved my cell phone from the car's middle console compartment. I planted it there before I entered Diamond's house not wanting to be bothered with any phone calls for the day. When I looked at my phone I had three missed calls from Nicole. I proceeded to check my messages as I expected Nicole had left me a few. As expected, the first message was from her stating the party last night was a success and she wanted to see me today. The second message from her was slightly frantic as she stated I was avoiding her. Finally, the third message was Nicole being irate saying she would simply mail me the cash she made from the party and didn't appreciate me using her.

"Why the hell can't her crazy ass get on with her life without me?" I asked myself out loud while looking at my phone. Then I put my eyes back on the road and continued driving. I wasn't in the mood for any of her mental shenanigans tonight, so I didn't even bother to return her call. Besides, it had been a while since we were intimate and I could tell in her voice she wanted some. Nicole indicating she was upset was just some reverse psychology shit she was always famous for. I brushed it off as Nicole just being crazy again.

By now, I was pulling into my condo's parking garage and glad I had made it back home safely. I decided I would spend the rest of the night catching up on a baseball game on ESPN. First thing Monday morning it was back to the grind of making a few sales calls trying to sell my remaining inventory. I also planned to put a strategy together for my consulting business and was overly excited about that.

After I parked my car, I decided to take the stairs to my condo on the twelfth floor. I stuffed myself like a hog back at Diamond's place and needed to burn off the extra calories. The last thing a needed now was a bulging gut at my age. By the time I got to the eighth floor in the stairwell my phone vibed.

"Oh God, please don't let this be crazy Nicole calling me again," I said aloud.

I pulled the phone from my hip holster and realized someone just sent me a text. By now, everyone knew I wasn't overly excited about receiving text messages. Clicking on the text, I noticed there was an attachment. When I opened the attachment I was shocked, surprised and pleased.

There she stood as sexy as a Greek goddess with a full backside view. Her body was fully unclothed and all she wore was a pair of brown suede BCBG boots that extended all the way above her knees. Her hands were strategically placed on her hips and she smiled while overlooking her left shoulder into the camera.

The text read: *Surprise! Hope u like what u c. I'd love 2 b ur "Boot Freak", Tameka.*

Tameka's body was banging sure enough, but I was trying to figure out how she got my phone number. I jogged the remaining flights of stairs and made it inside of my condo. Once there, I sat on the sofa still looking at Tameka's picture with a slight erection. Then I realized the moment at Diamond's salon when she asked to see my phone. Apparently, she must have dialed her own number from my phone. I sat there in the dark wondering what to do next.

Chapter 32

The first day of school had arrived quicker than I could have imagined. During the last week I spent more quality time with Christian by taking him to the movies, the Georgia Aquarium, and shopping in my neck of the woods at Lenox Mall. Even though the school he was attending required uniforms, I bought him extra clothes to wear anyway. When I was a kid his age everybody had a new pair of Air Jordan's for the first day of school and I felt obligated to keep the tradition going with my son.

You would have thought it was the first day of school for me, as I was overwhelmingly excited. I awoke before the sun even came up anxious to meet Diamond and Christian by 7:00 a.m. Even though his school was only fifteen minutes from Diamond's house, we wanted to arrive well before the eight o'clock start time.

As I travelled north on Georgia 400 again, I had to pass through the toll booth and deposit the required fifty cents. The car's driver in front of me obviously was searching for change to place in the toll machine and was holding up the line. I impatiently blew my horn as he finally made the deposit and drove off, but not before he honked back at me. I zipped through the toll and noticed all the cars in the southbound lane were stuck and not moving at all. Everybody from the suburbs were trying to make it into the city before the early morning commute. "Suckers," I said to myself as I continued traveling northbound. Didn't they realize now the surface streets were the best option to get into the overcrowded city by now.

When I arrived at Diamond's it was precisely 7:00 a.m. and she buzzed me through the security gate as before. By the time I pulled around to Diamond's home, Christian and her were coming out of the front door. He was dressed just like a studious school kid wearing khaki pants, a stripped button down shirt, and a tie to match. Attached to his back was a solid blue book bag and the white Air Jordan's I bought for him were on his feet. I parked in front of Diamond's townhome so I could greet them.

"Good morning, All-Star," I said. "Are you ready for your first day of school?"

"Yes sir," he replied smiling back.

"Good morning, baby," said Diamond

"Morning sweetheart."

We all got into my car and headed to Christian's school as Diamond gave me the directions. As expected, the traffic was heavy headed towards the school though we didn't have to take the interstate. On the way there, we stopped for a school bus picking up kids.

"Mom, why am I not riding the bus to school?

"Well, because Christian everything is still so new right now. Maybe by next year, we'll be able to let you ride the bus to school."

When we pulled up to the school, it was packed and busy as expected. There were buses pulling up letting kids off, parents with their kids in hand, and traffic being directed by school personnel. I parked in a designated area and we all walked towards the school.

Upon entering the school, we noticed other parents with their children attempting to walk them to their classroom. Diamond had already been given a tour by school administrators when she registered Christian and was somewhat familiar with the surroundings. I noticed how all the kids were neat and very presentable in their new uniforms and shoes. The school's atmosphere gave off a sense of discipline and responsibility.

As we walked down a narrow corridor trying to get Christian to his class before the eight o'clock deadline, Diamond noticed a woman moving frantically in the direction we were traveling. She was tall and dressed in a blue business suit carrying a handful of paperwork.

"Excuse me, hello Ms. Johnson," Diamond said stopping the woman.

"Hi," she replied with a smile and vibrant facial expression. "You're Ms. Graham from Chicago, right?"

"Yes, I see you still remembered me from a few weeks ago when I was registering my son for school here."

"Oh yes, dear, I hardly ever forget a face or name despite the countless number of parents I meet."

Ms. Johnson was the school's principal. She was an older woman with a few grey hairs showing. You could tell she enjoyed her job because of her warm and upbeat personality. She looked down at Christian and quickly struck up a conversation.

"So, I finally get to meet Christian in person," she said still smiling. "Well he looks just as handsome as the pictures you showed me Ms. Graham. Good morning, Christian, I'm Ms. Johnson the school principal. Are you excited about your first day of school?"

"Yes ma'am," he replied in a shy tone.

"Do you know who your teacher is?" she asked Christian.

"Yes ma'am, I do," he said with confident. "It's Ms. Anthony in room 106."

"That's right, Christian. I can already tell your going to be a one of our smartest fourth graders."

Diamond and I smiled and looked at Christian to let him know everything was going to be great with his new school. She could tell he had a hint of nervousness and rarely talked when he was not use to a particular surrounding. Ms. Johnson was making sure he felt comfortable and welcomed him at the same time.

"Well Christian, I'm actually headed right pass Ms. Anthony's classroom," Ms. Johnson exclaimed. "Would you like to walk with me there?"

"Yes ma'am," Christian responded. Then he took a step from us and joined Ms. Johnson on her side.

"Give me a hug and kiss Christian," said Diamond as she kneeled down towards him.

"Oh mom, you're going to embarrass me in front of the other kids."

"I don't care, you're my son and I love you. Besides, you're too young to be embarrassed and never too old to give your mother a hug and kiss."

Diamond and Christian hugged which seemed to be for an extended period of time. She kissed him as well, and he rejoined Ms. Johnson. Before they departed Ms. Johnson looked towards me to make an introduction. During the prior conversation, Diamond had unintentionally forgotten to introduce us.

"Hello sir, I don't believe we met before," she said. "I'm Ms. Johnson the school principal."

"Nice to meet you, Ms. Johnson," I replied. "I'm Damien." Then I extended my hand and received a firm handshake from her.

"I see the resemblance is quite obvious between you and your son, Christian," she said. "I know you're definitely proud of him."

My eyes widen as Ms. Johnson had me in an odd situation. Never before had anyone mentioned Christian being my son in his presence. I paused for a moment not knowing what to say as my facial expression showed it. At that point, Christian was looking right at me.

"Oh I'm sorry, did I say something in error?" Ms. Johnson asked.

"No, there's nothing wrong and you're right," I said. "I am the proudest father my son could have." Right then Christian looked into my eyes and smiled showing all his teeth. Even Diamond got into the act.

"Let's not keep Ms. Anthony waiting Christian," said Ms. Johnson. "Say your goodbyes and we'll be on our way."

"Bye mom," Christian said.

"Bye Christian, I love you," she shouted softly. "Don't forget I'll pick you up right after school today."

"Bye dad," he said waving.

"Goodbye son," I replied and waved back.

It was a great day to remember not only because it was Christian first day of school in Atlanta. This was the first time he actually called me "dad" and I called him "son."

Chapter 33

It was Friday the start of the long Labor Day weekend and I was glad it had arrived. Besides the signs of fall being only a few weeks away, the temperature was going to take a nosedive. Everyone was wishing for cooler weather as this summer was yet another scorcher for the record books. My inventory was almost depleted as I had managed to sell most of the new products I received lately from Mookie. It seemed like my hustling days were finally coming to an end but not before one last big weekend where I was sure to score big.

Diamond wanted me to stop by her salon today as it was scheduled to be packed with regulars and new clients. She told me earlier in the week women were sure to be getting their hair fried and dyed for plans on the long weekend. Plus, a number of her clients had been asking for me as well. After that, I promised to stop by for one final sales call since I was retiring from the business. I could also see Raphael since he had now moved out and I were missing all those signature dishes.

One of the reasons I stayed away from Diamond's salon was Tameka. Since she texted me that provocative photo, I was reluctant to call her back. I didn't want to cause waves between Diamond and I if she ever found out about Tameka, so I decided to avoid her advances altogether. The fact that Tameka worked for Diamond was a little bit too close for comfort. Drama was the last thing I was looking for now.

I arrived at Diamond's salon right after the noon lunch hour and I knew it would be packed. I barely found a parking space as I pulled up. Grabbing my short Gucci duffle bag full of goodies from the trunk, I headed inside to conquer a few sales. Tameka was sure to be positioned in her normal reception spot to greet me and I wondered how she would react to my presence.

"Hey boo boo!" shouted Raphael as I walked through the front door. He was obviously the first person to see me since his chair was closest to the entrance.

"What's going on cousin?" I replied. I held up my hand as to give him some dap but he wasn't having that. Raphael stepped away from his chair with a customer in it and gave me hug. "So how are things working out at your new place?"

"Honey, I love it! Nothing beats the location and the sense of my own independence in midtown Atlanta. So what have you been up to lately, Damien?"

"Just maintaining. I came by to sell a few items from my remaining inventory. After that, I'm out the business for good."

"So what do you have planned next?" he asked.

"I'm starting my own marketing consulting business and using the tax-free income I've made to cover my start up costs."

"I'm scared of you, Mr. Entrepreneur," he said. "Keep that money train going and create a job rather than take one."

"So where's Renee today?" I asked looking around the shop which was overly crowded. I even noticed a few women waving at me as their eyes we glued on my Gucci duffle bag.

"She's in her office in the back," he replied. "Well handle your business and I'll see you in a bit."

"Ok Raphael, I'll talk with your soon."

As I glimpsed over to the reception area, there was Tameka sitting watching me the whole time. She had a disgusted look on her face and seemed to be mad at me. It seemed as if she was looking right through me. There was no way to avoid her now as I made my way over to the reception desk. I figured I could at least be amicable to her.

"Hi Tameka, how are you today?"

"I guess that's a no," she said with a big attitude.

"No to what?"

"This sweet pussy you missed out on. I can't recall any guy ever turning this down." Right then Tameka stood up and revealed a short but tight and seductive dress she was wearing. She ran her hands over her hips, thighs, and ass. After that she stuck out her tongue and slowly rolled it over her top lip.

"I just didn't want any rift between you and Renee," I said. "Hope you can respect my decision."

"You mean, Diamond or should I say Ms. Graham," she responded. "I know all about her. Don't worry, I won't tell because one day you're going to wish you'd taste some of this sweet potato pie."

"No, I don't think so."

"We'll see about that."

Right then Diamond walked up as our conversation began to really get heated. I realized Tameka was nothing but bad news and messy.

"Hey, what are two talking about?" asked Diamond.

"Hello, baby," I said. Then I moved over to Diamond and gave her a kiss right there in front of Tameka to make her more jealous. "We're just talking about politics."

"Politics?" Diamond said confused.

"Yeah, you know how hot and heated that conversation can be," I said.

"Tameka, please go to the stockroom and bring out the new line of eco-green shampoo and conditioner I ordered last week," Diamond said. "I want the customers to see the new product line right here in the front display cases."

Tameka looked at me from head to toe and then moved to the back without saying a word. She didn't even bother to look at Diamond during her madness.

"What's wrong with her?" Diamond asked looking at me in a funny manner.

"Oh, it's nothing. She was just losing the conversation we were having right before you walked up."

"Well, the last thing I need is an employee with an attitude."

I spent the next hour in Diamond's salon letting the women have their way with my products. Once again, they were fascinated with my inventory, claiming they never saw such quality merchandise. I gave them a great deal they couldn't pass by. Hell, I'd figure I had nothing to lose since I needed to deplete my inventory in a hurry.

After I left Diamond's salon, I headed for a few salons on the Southside of the city. I figured my day would be more productive there. If I had enough time, maybe I would stop by Crystal's office just to see her smile.

Chapter 34

I was driving home from the bank on a windy morning. The weather was well into the fall season and I was glad of it. I had just cashed three unemployment benefit checks that had accumulated in my dresser drawer. Since I was hustling, I never really had a need for them but now that was going to stop. Until my consulting business got off the ground right, I had to make way with my benefit checks again. The checks were in no comparison to the money I was making every week hustling but it would suffice for now.

Most of my clients were surprised I had ceased my activities but respected my decision. They even offer to support my consulting business. I still had a few quirks to work out but luckily I had an abundance of contact numbers to solicit my business to. I wasn't worrying about it as I knew one way or another I would be successful, it was just a matter of marketing. Failure was not an option for me, especially right now.

I decided to stop in a grocery store and pick up some more Gatorade because I was totally out at home. I planned to get a good strenuous workout in today to help alleviant stress and tone up my body in all the right spots. Before I left the grocery store, I grabbed a bag of potatoes, pack of skinless chicken breasts, and head of lettuce for a salad. The other part of keeping in shape was proper diet and

I was a firm believer of that. I paid for the items through the self-checkout express lane then hopped back in my ride.

When I was about ten minutes from my condo, I received a call from Katrina. It had been over a month since our one night fling and she never called me back. I guess she shattered my three day rule concept and my ego was a little bruised. I wrote her off as just sex, nothing more nothing less. But now she was calling and I was curious as to why.

"Hello," I answered still remembering her cell number but not sounding anxious.

"Hello Damien, its Katrina. You still remember me?"

"How could I forget all that hot passionate sex we had. I thought you had forgotten about me."

"Oh no dear, I'm just swamped as usual in litigation madness here at work. Besides, it's about time for me to get some much needed heels for the change in season."

"Sorry Katrina, but I'm officially out of that racket for good. I sold the remains of my inventory a few weeks ago."

"Well, that's not what I wanted to hear," she said jokingly. "I guess it's back to Neiman Marcus for me."

"I actually started my own marketing consulting business," I said.

"How interesting and ironic you mentioned that," she said. "I'm actually calling to see if you would be my escort for a black-tie affair my firm is sponsoring. I could show you off to all my friends and you could use the event to network."

"Sounds like the perfect trade off. But you're comfortable with our age difference in public with your colleagues?"

"Please Damien, I didn't become this successful worrying about what people had to say or think. Besides, I have two grown sons nearly your age. I got to have a life too."

"Well, I'll take you up on the invite. So when and where is the event?"

"It's one week from this Saturday at eight o'clock in the W Hotel right next to Perimeter Mall. There will be a guy by the name of Julio from the tuxedo company calling you in a few days for your measurements. On the day of the event, I'll have a chauffeur pick you up and bring you to my house. We can then arrive at the gala together in style."

"I see you have everything planned out as usual," I said. "So, I'll see you next week for sure."

"I'll see you later, Damien. Oh, and by the way, good luck on your new business venture."

It was obvious Katrina wanted to have some fun with me and pass me off as her "boy toy" for the event. I'd go along for it since I was sure to make some business contacts. With all that money in one place for the evening, it was a definite hit for me. I would be a fool to turn down her offer.

By the time I made it to my condo, I was pumped and excited. I quickly placed the groceries in the fridge. What better way to celebrate good news than a good workout? In a matter of minutes, I had changed into my workout gear. As always, I grabbed a towel since I sweated profusely during my workout and a Gatorade. Once downstairs in the fitness center, I started with cardio exercises and jumped on the treadmill for forty-five minutes. While there I ran inclines and worked on steps. Throughout the workout I increased my speed periodically to gain maximum results.

After my cardio session, I went into the weight room. I worked on squats, curls, presses, and lifts for my upper and lower body. After spending nearly an hour in the weight room I felt like Hercules ready to conquer the world. I finished my weight room session by completing one hundred pushups and sits ups. Then I toweled off the sweat and drank my Gatorade in what seemed to be one giant gulp.

As tired as I was, I once again continued my ritual and took the stairs all the way to the twelfth floor. Once inside my condo, I opened a bottled water from the fridge and sucked it down my dry throat. I walked to my bathroom and turned on the shower to very hot. The hot water was a great muscle relaxer after a strenuous workout. There was no way I was taking a hot bath as it was just too feminine for me. Preparing to get undressed, I heard a knock at the door. Walking back to the front door with just my workout shorts on I looked through the peep hole.

"Who is it?" I yelled through the door noticing a white man in a delivery uniform.

"FedEx, sir," he shouted back. "I have a priority package for Damien Hardy."

The package was slightly bigger than an envelope and was tucked under his elbow as he had an electronic clipboard in the other hand. He patiently smiled and waited for my response.

"Just leave the package at the door, I'm about to jump in the shower."

"Sorry sir, no can do. This package needs a signature or it will be returned back to the sender."

"Who's the sender?" I asked still communicating through the door.

"It was sent from California," he replied.

Even though I was hot, sweaty, and musty from my workout I needed to open the door. If the package was from my grandmother and I never received it, she wouldn't let me hear the end of it. So right then, I decided to open the door.

"Just need your John Hancock right here, sir," said the delivery man pointing to the space on the clipboard while giving me the pen. "Have you been working out?"

"Yeah, just a little bit," I said while signing my name.

"Well, you look fabulous."

He gave me the package as I looked at him in a peculiar way wondering about his comment. Then he took the clipboard back out of my possession, handed me the package, and thanked me before making his way back towards the elevator. With the package in hand I turn around and shut the door behind me. Before the door closed a foot from the outside kept it ajar.

"Freeze! FBI, get your ass on the floor now!" said an unknown intimidating voice from behind me.

When I turned around there was a barrage of undercover agents wearing FBI jackets, with bullet proof vest, pointing their nine millimeter guns at me. I was shock like a deer caught in the headlights and couldn't move. My jaw dropped wide open and my hands went up in the air as the package fell to the floor.

"I said drop your ass to the floor!" yelled a burley black agent while I looked down the barrel of his Glock. Before I knew it, he pushed me to the floor onto my stomach, faced down with my arms still extended into the air.

"What the hell is going on here?" I screamed.

"Mr. Hardy, you're being detained for racketeering, purchase of stolen goods, and engaging in a terroristic enterprise," said the burly Black man. "My name is Agent Smith and you'll do as your told from this point on."

"What!" Racketeering, stolen goods, and terroristic enterprise, I'm from L.A. and have no idea what you're talking about."

"Agent Davis, get over here and cuff the subject," ordered Agent Smith.

Apparently, Agent Smith was the head nigga in charge as everyone was marching to his beat of the drum. When agent Davis came over he placed his knee firmly on my neck so I couldn't move. Then he took my arms from around my head and cuffed them behind my back. I noticed Agent Davis was the delivery man I had previously opened the door for.

"Wait a minute, where are you taking me?" I asked.

"You're being taken downtown into federal custody for questing," Agent Smith replied.

"Agent Smith, you guys got the wrong person here! This is a terrible mistake."

"We'll sort it all out downtown, Mr. Hardy. For now let's go." Agent Smith looked me over with a menacing smile and said, "yeah and you stink too." He then turned to the other agents and made them find me a pair of sneakers, tee shirt, and light jacket from my bedroom closet. After that, I was on my way downtown.

During my confinement in federal custody I was interrogated for nearly ten hours. I was asked everything from my beginnings in Los Angeles to most recent events in Atlanta. It was then I was informed the FBI had received an anonymous call. Apparently, the person said I was selling stolen designer goods and stockpiling them in my condo. The federal agents took the information seriously because terrorist groups were known to front their causes this way. Thus, the federal agency was compelled to follow up on the tip. Of course, I cleared all the allegations during questioning and kept a poker face.

As for the package that was shipped to me, I was ordered to open it while in the interview room. The Feds were able to intercept the package from the same anonymous caller. When I opened the package there inside were various cut-out comic strips from different newspapers. All the comic strip characters were laughing to suggest a specific theme of toying with me. I simply got it that whoever did this wanted me to know they were having the last laugh.

Even the Feds were more perplexed about the cut-out comic strips as they scratched their heads. They took the evidence away and dusted them for prints but came up empty. The person who sent the package took every precaution not to leave any clues.

The Feds even had access to my bank records and tried to get me to admit to some wrongdoing that just didn't exist. All my financial activity showed no significant deposits or withdrawals to suggest any sort of illegal activity. To make matters worse, my cell phone records were already in their possession but revealed nothing as well. I guess the final straw was how they searched my vehicle while I was being questioned and came up empty again.

One thing I learned early in the hustle game was to always cover your tracks no matter what. I always used cash and never deposited any amount of money into my bank account that couldn't be justified. As for my cell and business, it just didn't mix. The Feds had a record of my personal cell phone but not the one I used for business. I kept an untraceable pre-paid cell phone hidden and it didn't even have my real name assigned to it. In all, the Feds were a day late and a dollar short. They were all dressed up with no place to go and I knew it but remained calm.

"Well Mr. Hardy, it seems as if you checked out clean for now," said Agent Smith as he reentered the interview room with a sense of disappointment. "But I just don't believe it. You better watch your every move boy, because I'm keeping my eye you."

"So I'm cleared to go?" I asked.

"All cleared," he exclaimed. "You're free to walk out the front door and take your damn package with you."

When I stumbled outside the federal building downtown, it was pitch dark and almost midnight. I was mentally drained, embarrassed, and simply pissed off at all that had transpired. I quickly walked to the Five Points Marta Station across from Underground Atlanta and jumped on a train to Buckhead.

When I reached the Buckhead Marta Station, I zipped up my jacket and prepared for the walk to my condo a few blocks away. I ditched the package in a nearby trash can with a frown on my face at the same time. I knew all along who the anonymous caller and package was from. It had to be that crazy ass Nicole up to her antics again. "Damn it," I said out loud maintaining a steady walk. I thought to myself, how could she do that to me?

Chapter 35

It had been a few days since my acquaintance with the Feds as I looked over the city from my balcony on a bright Sunday morning. The only plans I had for the day was watching NFL games. Even though I was an avid baseball fan, football was my first love. Watching games on Sundays had now been something I waited for all week long since the season was underway. I had invited Mookie and Raphael over for the day. Both were well aware now of what Nicole had put me through. Raphael, who didn't care for football, offered to cook us a luxurious dinner we would be proud of.

Without hesitation, I changed my locks and cell phone number the day after the incident. Nicole never had a key to my place but I wasn't taking any chances with her. I also put my building's security on notice for any suspicious women who fit her description. Even though she owed me a few stacks, I had written her off as bad debt. This was something I should have done a long time ago.

The first game started at one o'clock and Mookie arrived just in time for the opening kickoff. My favorite team, the Dolphins, was hosting the Falcons and I planned to watch every minute.

"What's up, Damien," said Mookie as I opened the front door after hearing the doorbell ring.

"What's up, Mookie," I replied glad to see my friend. We gave each other our customary dap and hug. "C'mon in man and have a seat, the game is about to start.

Mookie made himself at home on the sofa in front of the flat screen TV. It was the first time he had ever been to my place. I took a seat in the recliner, so I would be more comfortable watching the game.

"Nice place you got here, Damien. It's good to see you living like white folks all the way up here in Buckhead."

"C'mon Mookie, you know brothers now live on this side of town."

"Yeah, I'm just messing with you. I guess I still remember this area like it use to be back in the day. Man, I can't believe that woman would set you up like that. Are you sure it was her?"

"Hell yeah, Mookie. I put all the pieces of the puzzle together and everything pointed to Nicole. Besides, no one knows where I live or my routine as much as she did."

"I guess you can't be too careful with these women or put that whip on them," he said laughing. "Take it as a lesson learned and move on."

"I could not have agreed with you more," I exclaimed. Even though she still owed me money, I'll just have to take the loss."

"Like they say, easy come easy go," said Mookie.

"Yeah, but I'm going to miss him cause I loved him to death."

"You mean you're going to miss her."

"No, I mean him."

"Him! What are you talking about Damien? Don't tell me you're on some down low shit."

"No way, you know I love women. But I love him more."

"So who is this him character?" he asked.

"Ben," I replied.

"Ben who?"

"Benjamin Franklin!" We both burst out laughing as Mookie finally caught what I was saying.

"So how are things working out with the new gig?" I asked.

"I love it," he replied. "The staff is cool and the environment is just what I needed, a breath of fresh air. I even ran into my old high school assistant coach from Southwest DeKalb."

"Oh yeah."

"That's right. I told him what I was doing for the kids in the community and he even offered me a part time position as a strength and conditioning coach for the football team."

"Seems like everything is working out for the best," I said. "So how are things with you and Nadine?"

"She a God sent, Damien. It's so serious now, I'm thinking about going to the next level with her."

"Don't tell me you're thinking about that dreaded word."

"I've been giving it some serious thought and you ought to as well. You know your roster won't be filled up forever."

"So how do you really know when you're in love?" I asked. "How do you know when she is that woman you were meant to be with for the rest of your life?"

"Man, I can't even put it into words but you will know when it happens," he replied. "When that special person comes in your life you can't live without them. It's a great feeling bro."

I was way ahead of Mookie and definitely knew what he was talking about. The feeling he was speaking about only comes once or twice in your lifetime. The first time I felt it was when I was so in love with Crystal. Others would argue, I was too young to know what true love felt like but I knew. Now I was harboring those same feelings for Diamond that I once had for Crystal. But on the flip side there was still a small piece of me that still loved Crystal no matter what. My dilemma now was that I had to choose one of them.

By halftime our conversation was interrupted by the doorbell. I knew it had to be no one but Raphael. My hunger was becoming noticeable as I skipped breakfast as I normally did. I was anxious to hear what dish Raphael had in store for us today. When I looked through the peep hole it was him smiling with a grocery bag in his hand. I opened the door with no reluctance.

"Hey boo boo!" he yelled while walking into the foyer.

"Glad you made it and so is my stomach," I said as he gave me a hug and a fake kiss to both cheeks.

Raphael remained to keep it real no matter what. He was dressed in attire that fitted more for an equestrian event rather than Sunday dinner. His cheerful mood overshadowed his always present flamboyant attitude. But I had gotten use to his style by now as he was just being himself and loving it.

"Damien, I can't believe that trick had the audacity to try to set you up. And to think I hung out with her back stabbing, Jimmy Choo heel wearing ass."

"Don't even sweat it, cousin. It's water under the bridge and negative energy to keep thinking about it. Why don't you put the bag of groceries down in the kitchen so I can introduce you to someone?"

Raphael tiptoed into the kitchen as not to mark up the hardwood floor with the heels from the boots he was wearing. After he placed the contents of the bag on the kitchen counter, he rejoined me in the foyer. Then we walked into the living room where Mookie was consumed in the second half of the game.

"Mookie, I just wanted to introduce you to my cousin. Mookie this is Raphael, Raphael this is Mookie."

"What's up, man," Mookie said while he paused looking at Raphael. Instantly, he knew Raphael was a little different, and then turned his head back towards the TV.

"Haaaayy!" Raphael commented in a sultry voice. "Damien, you always had friends that were athletic and built like a tank which I like. I use to get so hot and bothered watching your baseball buddies during practice back in high school."

"So what's for dinner?" I asked interrupting Raphael before he got carried away with his imagination. By now, Mookie was shaking his head still looking at the TV, trying not to laugh.

"Honey, we're having Cornish hen, sauté red potatoes, and asparagus. Of course, everything is fresh and organic."

"That sound tasty," I said. "Well, I'll let you get your cook on while we watch football."

"Oh no, you know I don't do football," he said. I brought my iPod so it will be just me and Luther in the kitchen while I sip on a glass of Chardonnay."

By the time dinner was ready the second football game was almost over. I was beyond hungry and so was Mookie. But just as Raphael promised the meal was fabulous and worth the wait. Even Mookie was impressed and had to give Raphael his props. After dinner, Raphael cleaned the kitchen and made his way back to midtown Atlanta as he had an early day at the salon in the morning. Mookie and I sat in the living room, with our bellies stuffed, getting ready to watch the scheduled prime time night game.

Chapter 36

I was sharp as a tack, as my grandmother use to say, looking in the mirror at myself. I was wearing my tailored fit neatly pressed tuxedo prepared to meet with Katrina. It was amazing how well my tuxedo fit being that I could hardly understand Julio's accent when he called me for my measurements. Apparently, he understood me just fine which resulted in a superb-fitting outfit. I shouldn't have second guessed the tailor Katrina sent me to because with money comes quality.

Pulling away from the mirror, I noticed it was almost seven o'clock. "Where is this driver?" I asked myself impatiently. The driver Katrina hired to pick me up was to contact me no later than an hour before the event. This way, he would still have time to pick Katrina up in Alpharetta then chauffer us to the event together. Unlike some of the events I went to this one wasn't on CP time. So if the event started at eight that's what time it began. I began to pace my living room floor in my condo when I received a call on my cell phone.

"Hello," I answered.

"Yes sir, may I speak with Mr. Damien Hardy?" said the older distinctive voice on the other end in a British accent.

"This is Damien."

"Hello Mr. Hardy, I'm Theodore with Elite Driving Services. Ms. Hope retained our services for the evening and I've been advised to pick you up for the black-tie event."

"Yes, I was waiting for you to arrive."

"Please forgive me for any discomfort you may have incurred, sir. I am actually parked in front of your building now."

"Fine, I'll be right down Theodore." His accent caught me off guard as I never heard anyone speak like that in all my years living in Atlanta.

"Shall you require me to escort you downstairs to the vehicle, sir?"

"Oh, that's not needed. I should be able to find you just fine."

"Very well, sir," he said. "I'll await your presence downstairs in front of the vehicle."

As I hung up, I took one final look at myself in the mirror again. I tugged on my shirt sleeves a little to make sure my cufflinks would show. Then I straighten my tie one last time and buttoned my tuxedo jacket. Whisking out the door, I noticed it was exactly seven o'clock on my watch.

When I arrived downstairs and the elevator doors opened, I quickly made my way to the front door entrance. As I walked forward, I noticed my building security guard on duty and gave him a friendly nod. He gestured back by raising his hand but I could see his eyebrows rise as he noticed my outfit. Already, I could see Theodore in front of the black Range Rover prominently standing waiting for me. He too was dressed in a tuxedo and had a freshly clean shaven face.

"You must be Mr. Hardy, I presume," he said as I walked up to the vehicle.

"Indeed I am."

"Glad to meet your acquaintance, sir," he said while opening the rear door to the Range Rover. "Please have a seat and we'll be ready to depart."

"Thank you, Theodore."

When I took my seat in the back of the vehicle, I easily noticed the Range Rover was custom made. It was classy but not too flashy. There wasn't a dirty spot on the vehicle inside or out. The limo tint ensured whoever was sitting in the back would have complete privacy from any unwanted on-lookers. As Theodore closed my door and made his way to the drivers' side seat, I observed a small bar within the back seat area. I even noticed the noisy security guard taking a glimpse of me before we pulled off.

"Sir, I've set the vehicle's GPS for Ms. Hope's residence and we shall arrive there in less than twenty minutes," he said after sitting in the drivers' seat placing his seatbelt on. "While you were coming downstairs I took the liberty of calling her advising of our anticipated arrival."

"Sounds like a plan, Theodore," I said.

"You'll notice an array of spirits within your confinement sir," he said while we pulled away from the building. "Do not hesitate to wet your palate if you choose to do so."

By the time we got on the interstate, I took Theodore up on his offer and gladly fixed myself a glass of cognac with ginger ale. I even chuckled to myself in awe of the British accent driver but was impressed. One thing about Katrina was for sure, she didn't cut corners and knew about class. It was no telling what was in store for the night once I met with her network of friends. Just as Theodore said we made it to Katrina's mini mansion within twenty minutes. I had just finished my drink and popped a piece of peppermint in my mouth. I was a bit more relaxed now looking forward to seeing her.

"As you can see sir we have arrived at Ms. Hope's residence. If you could be so kind to wait, I'll see if she is ready."

"Sure thing, Theodore."

Theodore exited the vehicle with the engine running as he made his way to Katrina's front door. After he climbed the long brick stairs to the front door, he promptly rang the doorbell. Within a few seconds he disappeared into the house as I looked from the back seat of the Range Rover. I thought about making myself another drink but decided to wait. I still had to make a good impression with Katrina's friends and I didn't want to smell like alcohol.

After a few minutes of me sitting in the vehicle, Katrina and Theodore appeared at the front door. She was dressed sophisticated and looked radiant as ever as Theodore walked her down the long brick steps. She held on to his elbow gracefully showing off her evening dress. Her hair was styled for the classy event displaying her diamond earrings that had to be at least a few carats with all the bling. Her necklace which was full of diamonds as well complimented her earrings too. Katrina was dressed to impressed and wanted everyone to know it, including me.

"Hello gorgeous," I said as Theodore opened the back door of the Range Rover for Katrina. I extended my hand as well so she would be comfortable getting in.

"Hi handsome," she replied sitting close to me. "Well don't you look like a true gentleman.

"What can I say? Your tailor Julio did a great job."

"Well, like the saying goes, a man definitely makes the clothes and you're no exception," said Katrina.

As Theodore drove off smoothly, I offered to make Katrina a drink but she declined. She insisted on champagne once we arrived at the event. By eight o'clock on the dot we arrived at the W Hotel as planned. There were quite a few vehicles in front of ours as Theodore attempted to maneuver towards the entrance. I could see a few couples arriving in everything from high end cars to flashy sports vehicles. All the women were fabulously dressed with their dates in tuxedos, of course. When our vehicle finally arrived at the front entrance, there was a valet who opened Katrina's rear door and gave a warm welcome assisting her out. Quickly, I joined her on the other side of the vehicle where our arms intertwined and we walked forward making a grand entrance.

We spent the next few hours mingling as Katrina introduced me to so many people I lost count. After feeling everyone out and finding out who was who, I made a few successful sales pitch for my consulting business. You know when you're in a room full of money when there is no reluctance to help you. On more than one occasion, a few businessmen offered to utilize my services by just me knowing and being there with Katrina. The old motto of "who you know not what you know" was true in this case.

Katrina on the other hand had a few glasses of champagne by now and was feeling good. On one occasion, we got separated and I caught her proudly pointing me out to her girlfriends. It was as if she was basking in the prize catch of the day as her girlfriends gave her the stamp of approval. When we reconnected I played it off as if I didn't notice a thing. She could point me out, show me off, and introduce me to whomever. I really didn't care just as long as I completed my agenda of making money through new contacts.

"Come on Damien, let's get out of here."

"Why so early?" I asked. "Besides, it's barley after ten o'clock and the night is just getting started. I still want to meet a few more contacts of yours."

"Because I'm tipsy and horny as hell," she exclaimed. "You'll do great with the contacts I introduced you to because they're real money players. Besides, I already gave my donation to the event and showed you off enough. Now I need you to fuck the shit out of me like last time."

Katrina was in her demanding mood again but I wasn't going to argue with her. Since she earned the right for me to sex her down even if I had lost the interest altogether. I felt obligated to give her what she wanted since she did help me out with networking. I left Katrina in the hotel's ballroom and went outside to find Theodore. He was in a group with the other valets chatting away in his British accent. I could tell they were enjoying his accent as he commanded the group's attentiveness. I raised my hand to gain his attention and right on cue he looked towards me. He nodded his head as to say "right away, sir" and I knew he would bring the Range Rover around.

As I turned and made my way back into the W Hotel, I received an incoming text message on my BlackBerry. The message read: *Please come over ASAP. It's an emergency!* The text was from Crystal and she even left her address within the text message. I knew Crystal wouldn't have contacted me if she really didn't need me. Before I made it back inside the ballroom where Katrina was, I texted Crystal back. My response read: *I'm on my way!*

By now, Katrina was really feeling good as she had another glass of champagne in her hand. I quickly grabbed her arm as we made our way through the crowd and walked back towards the front entrance. I made her hold onto my arm, as if we were in love, otherwise she would have been stumbling all over the place. When we finally reached the Range Rover, Theodore already had the rear door open waiting for us. We got in quickly and I knew I had to get to Crystal fast. As Theodore drove down Ashford-Dunwoody Road past Perimeter Mall, Katrina managed to gain her composure and blurt out a comment.

"Take us to my place, Theodore," she said with a slur speech.

"Yes ma'am, as you wish."

"Actually Theodore, you can drop me off at my place first," I said.

"I am sorry, sir," he remarked.

"I won't be going over to Ms. Hope's place with her tonight."

"Very well, sir, as you wish."

My request caught Katrina totally off guard as she looked at me in confusion. She even managed to conjure up a smirk on her face by now.

"So what's the meaning of this, Damien? Why aren't you coming home with me tonight?

"It's unexpected business I have to take care of," I replied back quickly.

"If you think I'm going to believe that lame excuse you got to be crazy!" By now Katrina was nearly screaming. "I guess one of your lady friends decided to give you a call while we were at the event. You mean to tell me she treats you better than me?"

I didn't even attempt to answer her question but gave her the silent treatment instead and looked out my passenger window. Sometimes silence is the best way to battle in an argument, especially when the person you're talking to is drunk. Within ten minutes we had arrived in front of my building and Katrina had damn nearly bit her tongue off trying to keep from exploding into a full blown argument with me.

"Here we are sir, as you wished," Theodore said. "We are at your place of residence. Enjoy the rest of your evening."

"You do the same, Theodore. It was pleasure meeting you."

"Likewise, sir," he replied.

"After all I did for you this evening, and this is how you repay me?" Katrina asked with an attitude as I attempted to make my way out the vehicle.

"Sorry Katrina, you just don't understand and besides I'm way bigger than being your boy toy for the night. Money can't buy you everything. Didn't they teach you that in law school?"

By now, I was outside the vehicle with the rear passenger door still partially open. Theodore kept his composure and continued to look forward as if he wasn't hearing a word of our heated conversation. I guess my remark struck a nerve because her face turned red as a tomato.

"Fuck you, Damien!"

"How original from someone who is suppose to be so classy and successful," I said shaking my head.

"Despite what you think, I can have any man I want in Atlanta with or without my money and status," she yelled back.

"Oh, I forgot to tell you one thing before I go."

"What is it now?" she shouted.

"Hope you charged your batteries before you left home!"

Before she could respond to my remark, I slammed the rear door of the Range Rover. Then I made a quick run for my building's parking garage.

Chapter 37

It was right around eleven o'clock when I reached Crystal's home. I tried to call her once I left Buckhead but her phone was off. Obviously, there was something major going on. I thought about placing a call to 911 but who was I fooling. I had a better chance of reaching Crystal well before 911 would even answer their lines. My GPS took me exactly where she lived on the better, yet pricy, neighborhood off Cascade Road. As I imagined the homes were images of well-to-do people.

Crystal's white S550 was parked in her driveway and I promptly parked behind it. When I arrived at her front door I noticed all the lights were off in the home. Then I rang the doorbell praying for a response. After continued silence, I eagerly rang the doorbell once again and still no answer.

"Crystal, it's me Damien," I shouted while banging on the front door with my fist. "Hey are you alright in there?"

I banged on the door again and still there was no reply from Crystal. Frantically, I reached for my BlackBerry and dialed Crystal's cell phone hoping to reach her. But once again, my call went straight to her voice mail. At that moment, it occurred to me I ought to try turning the door knob. Before I touched the door knob, I covered my hand with a portion of my jacket. I read about this technique in an old

Dick Tracy comic strip when I was a kid. The purpose was to never leave any fingerprints at the scene. At this point, I didn't know what to expect on the inside of Crystal's home. Surprisingly, the door opened once I turned the knob.

Once inside the home, I noticed a small flicker of light in the distance around the corner. It was the only light that illuminated the home which was pitch black dark inside. There was also soft music playing but I couldn't quite make out who was the artist. I balled my fists tight and prepared for the worst as I walked forward towards the glow of light. When I finally came up to the wall to turn the corner I took one deep breath and moved forward.

What I saw was quite shocking. There was Crystal sitting there with her legs crossed half-way naked in a white Victoria Secret outfit staring right at me. Rose petals littered the room's floor and one single scented candle was burning. The song playing was "Turn off the Lights" by Teddy Pendergrass which was an old school classic.

"So what took you so long?" she asked taking a sip of wine out a glass flute in her hand. Then she rose off the plush chair she was sitting in and walked towards me. "You like what you see?"

My jaw was nearing hanging wide open as I stared at Crystal's coke bottle figure. I finally was able to pull myself together and answer "hell yeah."

"I have a lot of making up to do with you after all these years," she said standing in front of me. "What better way than to start right now. I know I caused you much pain, but I promise to make it all go away after tonight." She grabbed my hand and placed it on her waist and moved forward to kiss me.

We kissed softly as I rubbed my hand down her lower back towards her ass then stopped. Instantly, all the memories of us flashed in my head like a light bulb going off and on. Even the feeling for her was different right then.

"Wait a minute Crystal, this isn't right between us."

"What do you mean, Damien?"

"I mean what we had long ago was just that, what we had."

"But we can make it better than that," she said. "One mishap doesn't outweigh all the great times we had together."

"Yes it does sweetheart," I said while pushing away from her. "There will always be a place in my heart for you, but I can never love you the same. So instead of shortchanging you, I rather move on where my heart belongs."

"And where is that?"

I didn't even answer her after that but knew I had to get out of there. "Look, I got to go, just believe in everything I just said and take care." I turned and walked towards the front door beginning my exodus. She followed me to the front door and then watched me get into my car. After I maneuvered out her driveway, I didn't even look back but pressed the accelerator fast. I was on my way to be with the woman I truly loved.

Chapter 38

It was almost midnight as I travelled on I-285 headed northbound. I thought about what just happened and whether or not I made the right decision. Then I remembered my most recent conversation with Mookie when he said, "I would know when that special person was right for me." That special person was Diamond and my heart was gravitating towards her even more. Never in my life had I given something so much thought right then and I wasn't going to let her slip out of my life again. My starting five didn't exist to me anymore and I really didn't care. As far as I was concern to hell with it! Rookies eventually mature to veterans and then veterans retire at some point. I wasn't going to be the old coach left standing with the ball and no one to play with.

I picked up my BlackBerry, while I was driving, and decided to call Diamond immediately. After a couple of rings she finally picked up her phone.

"Hello," answered Diamond in her sexy relaxed voice.

"Hey Diamond, it's Damien. Are you still awake?"

"Yes baby, Christian and I just finished watching a movie. He's knocked out now sleeping next to me on the sofa."

"Well, I wanted to come by and see you."

"Okay, that's fine, Damien. I'll go ahead and lay Christian down in his bed."

"But don't tuck him in," I said. "I want to do that when I get there."

"Aw, you're such a sweet daddy."

"I know."

We both chuckled at my last comment as I told Diamond I would be there shortly. After I hung up with her, I'd already made it to the toll booth on Georgia 400. It would now only be a matter of minutes before I reached my destination.

As usual, Diamond buzzed me into the gated townhome community once I arrived. Like before her garage door was opened and I quickly pulled into what seemed to be my designated spot. Once the garage door closed behind my car, I raced inside the house and up the first flight of stairs. When I reached the second floor Diamond was there waiting for me. She was simply dressed in boy shorts, a rhinestone contoured-fitting Bebe tee shirt, and her hair was pulled back in a ponytail. Even dressed down she looked sexy.

"Hi baby," said Diamond as I walked up to her. Without responding I gave her a smooth kiss and a long hug. "Well what was all that for?"

"I just missed you and needed to show you how much," I replied back as we came out of our embrace.

"Now look at you all dressed up, like you're on the cover of *GQ Magazine*. So where have you been tonight?"

"Nowhere spectacular," I said smiling at Diamond's remark. "I just had to attend a business function earlier this evening. So where is Christian?"

"He's upstairs in his room, I just laid him down."

"C'mon I want to see my son," I said as I grabbed Diamond's hand.

We made it all the way to Christian's room on the third floor of the townhome, where his bedroom door was partially open. Diamond turned on the hall light so it would resonate into his room as I opened the door more. There he was sleeping like a baby in his baseball pajamas with the covers slightly off of him. I bent down and kissed him on his cheek and whispered, "I love you son," into his ear while Diamond stood by the door. Then ever so carefully, I pulled the covers up to his shoulders.

"Dad, is that you?" he asked still half-way asleep.

"Yes All-Star. Now go back to sleep and I'll see you in the morning."

Diamond and I made our way back downstairs and retired to the living room area which was pitch dark. I plopped down on her soft sofa, seeking rest and relaxation, as I was drained physically and mentally from the night. While there, I took off my jacket and tie then slipped off my shoes. Diamond made her way into the kitchen then returned with two wine glasses filled with Moscato. She lit a few scented candles and press play on the stereo compact disc player which was hooked up to surround sound.

"So what are you playing now?" I asked taking a sip of wine.

"Shhh, it's a surprise," she said. "Let me see if you remember this tune."

When the music came on it was the 80's classic hit "Fire and Desire" by Rick James featuring Teena Marie. The song itself was iconic back then and still today. It symbolized two individual's love for each other, just like Diamond and I had.

"Diamond, you went way old school on me with that hit."

"Do you remember this song and where you first heard it with me?"

"Yeah, it was at your place ten years ago in the Grandview. It was on that old school love mix cd you were playing."

"That's right, Damien. Can you believe this is still the same cd?"

"What!"

"Yes, baby, I saved it after all these years. C'mon Damien get up and dance with me, I love this song."

Diamond took me by my arm as I stood up next to her and we embraced. I placed my hands softly on her hips while she maneuvered her arms around my shoulders and neck. We slow danced to the smooth melody until the lyrics came on. Then I pretended to be Rick James and recited the first verse singing to Diamond while looking straight into her eyes:

Wow
Its really good to see you again, baby
And I must admit you're looking very, very, very nice these days
I guess life must be treating you well
Oh me
Well, I've just been doin' the same ol' thing I've always been doin'

You know, I've got a new lady now
And it's a little different then it was when I was with you
You know, I think back to when we met
The way I use to be and the wild way I use to act
But more than that, I think of how you changed me with your love
and sensitivity
Remember when I use to

When the first verse was over I dropped to one knee to add a little melodrama for the recital. I spread both of my arms open while Diamond smiled with emotions, then I sang the hook:

Love them and leave them
That's what I used to do
Use and abuse them
Then I laid eyes on you

It was pain before pleasure
That was my claim to fame
With every measure, baby
Tasted teardrop stains, yeah

I was cold as ice long ago, baby, baby
I wasn't very, very, very nice, you know
Sugar, sugar, sugar
Then I kissed your lips

And you turned on my fire, baby
And you burn me up within your flame
Took me a little higher
Made me live again

You turned on my fire, baby
Then you showed me what a love could do
Fire and desire, baby
Feel it comin' through

By the time the hook had ended I raised back up to my feet where Diamond kissed me with a passion. She was crying tears of joy and so was I. We continued to slow dance while the rest of song played.

"Oh, Damien, I really do love you."

"I love you more, Diamond," I said softly. "And baby I just want us to spend the rest of our lives together."

When the hook for the song came back up again we both sang it together. For that moment in time, I was her Rick James and she was my Teena Marie.